2-29-20

BILLY

ALBERT FRENCH

BILLY

VIKING

VIKING
Published by the Penguin Group
Penguin Books USA Inc., 375 Hudson Street,
New York, New York 10014, U.S.A.
Penguin Books Ltd, 27 Wrights Lane,
London W8 5TZ, England
Penguin Books Australia Ltd, Ringwood,
Victoria, Australia
Penguin Books Canada Ltd, 10 Alcorn Avenue,
Toronto, Ontario, Canada M4V 3B2
Penguin Books (N.Z.) Ltd, 182–190 Wairau Road,
Auckland 10, New Zealand

Penguin Books Ltd, Registered Offices:
Harmondsworth, Middlesex, England

First published in 1993 by Viking Penguin,
a division of Penguin Books USA Inc.

3 5 7 9 10 8 6 4 2

PUBLISHER'S NOTE
This is a work of fiction. Names, characters,
places, and incidents either are the
product of the author's imagination or
are used fictitiously.

LIBRARY OF CONGRESS CATALOGING IN PUBLICATION DATA
French, Albert
Billy / Albert French.
p.   cm.
ISBN 0-670-85013-6
I. Title.
PS3556.R3948B5   1993
813'.54—dc20   93-14676

Printed in the United States of America
Set in Bodoni Book
Designed by Lucy Albanese

To my
mother and father
Martha and *Harry*
to my sisters
Cheryl and *Stacie*
gentle hearts that always sailed
to me in my storms

and to my cousin
John
and his wife, *Judy*
who always kept their light on

". . . through many dangers, toils and snares . . ."

—JOHN NEWTON
"Amazing Grace"
1750?

ACKNOWLEDGMENTS

Thanks to
Sarah Chalfant
who always saw the light when
I had closed my eyes.
Barry and *Myrna Paris*
for your help in the night.

And then to
Dawn Seferian
who took the dream out of the night
and put it in the sunlight.

BILLY

1

Out there by Til Hatcher's farm, especially in them pickin fields, it was hot. If it ain't rained it got dusty too. Them wagons comin back from them pickin fields be that dusty color, same color of that red dirty road they be rollin on. Big Jake be lookin sorta funny sometimes, he be sittin high up in the back of that wagon just a sweatin so much that road dust be turnin to mud as soon as it be hittin his face. Miss Cinder be the same way, except she be hafe tryin to get undressed, she be havin her dress all loose and hafe unbuttoned like she tryin to get some air on her to dry up some of that pickin sweat, but she be gittin that road dust stuck on her too. Cinder always thinkin and actin like she too good, too pretty to be out in them fields. She knows folks a lookin at her, her dress hafe off and all, but she don't care and if she does she ain't showin it.

Most of the time Big Jake be singin, sometimes everybody in the wagon be singin cept Cinder, pickin time be over, and that can be worth singin about. Mister Pete, he used to be the one singin all the time, singin and chantin them pickin songs. That's one thing that old man could do was sing all day, be singin more than he be pickin. He was old, rememberin a lot of things, always talkin about when them Yankee soldiers come ridin through. He said he seen em, he said he was down by the Catfish Creek, he and his brother be down there, he said he had a brother, he said he seen them soldiers just a comin on them big brown horses wit all that dust a trailin em. He say he ran up in them trees by Missy Jane's and them soldiers just ride on by, ain't paid him no mind. He's dead now, wasn't nothin but skin and bone, didn't even know how old he was, found him sittin up there in that old chair he sit at, he was just as dead as anything could be. Big Jake sorta be doin the singin now, but he don't sing all the time.

Nighttime be hot too, but different than the days, pickin time be over, everybody be sittin outside, too hot to be inside them shacks, bugs be just a bitin. Some folks be sittin, hearin all that music comin from down LeRoy's place, that music be just a jumpin. You be over LeRoy's place you be seein everything. Lucy Mae, she be dancin, she be movin her butt all up in Shorty. Shorty be happy, just a smilin and dancin too. Sweat be so thick on folks it be lookin like slime, be shinin too.

Sometimes Cinder be over LeRoy's place, get some of that corn liquor in her and dance too. She be twistin and turnin just like a snake, have her hands all up in that long black Indian hair she got. Folks stop watchin Lucy Mae, start watchin

Cinder. Everybody be watchin her, but she don't smile, just have that evil look in her eyes like when she sittin in the back of that hot pickin-wagon wit all that dust gittin on her.

Pickin fields, hot days, Mississippi suns, just seem to be there. Been there all the time. Banes County was just Banes County. Summer nineteen thirty and seven was just summer and hot, dusty too if it ain't rained good. Folks didn't come to Banes much, didn't come to stay at all, just pass through like them Yankee soldiers Mister Pete talked about seein. Folks in Banes were not fightin to get out. They had their ways, and movin quick or far wasn't any of them. Banes folk just change with age some, then just die. Most folks didn't count days, no sense in that, remember things by the spring of the year, floodin time. "Let's see . . . Mister Pete . . . he be dead just before a spring ago. . . ."

Sometimes the train stops down in town at the station, sometimes folks get off, get on, but most of the time the train just be stoppin to get some water, sit there on them tracks steamin up the place, then start to move, wiggle back and forth till it get goin, then everything be just the same way before the train came. Biggest thing in town was the courthouse, Banes bein the county seat, town folks sorta looked forward to seein one another sooner or later down by the courthouse. Most of the shops were on Front Street, the shoppin stores, hair-cuttin shop, Rosey Gray's restaurant, and Mason's saw-yard down on the other end of the street. On the back streets, folks lived, most did their livin sittin on the porch, talkin about their yesterdays. Banes had its Saturday nights and its Saturday-night places. Folks, mostly them young boys, come in from all over, get liquored up, start chasin them Saturday-night women, kept Sheriff Tom busy.

Sheriff Tom was as mean as he was big, except when he get drunk, and then he look funny, had that sheriff hat sittin so far back on his head you wondered how it stayed on, and that pistol belt be all twisted, had that gun hangin right down between his legs, some folks be hopin it go off one time down there. Sheriff Tom is mean. Shot that old man Henry's boy Sam again after he already shot him once, shot him again right in the head, then shot at them dogs that were barkin. Old man Henry's Sam was drinkin and stealin, come at Sheriff Tom with one of them corn-liquor bottles. Happened right down by the tracks at the end of Dillion Street.

At the end of Dillion Street and on the other side of the Catfish Creek bridge, most of the colored folks lived, been livin down there since folks could remember. Folks called it the Patch. The Patch had that one road runnin down there. Hot days that road be dusty, rain time it be just a muddy stream, just as mucky as a old horse stall. Them shacks and sheds down there seem to be all over the place, hafe of them the wood so rotten they look like big old termite logs, them kind you kick and they fall all apart. Folks down there kept to their ways most of the time, worked them pickin fields. Some of them had a little land up behind them shacks, but that Patch land was so hacked at, it just looked like bare dusty ground, just like that Patch Road.

Town folks and Patch folks hadn't started talkin about Billy Lee Turner yet. Billy Lee was Cinder's boy, the only thing that woman cared about. Town folks didn't know Billy Lee from any other of them Patch darky children. Patch folks knew Billy Lee was Cinder's boy and sorta thought he was that Otis's boy, had some of them Otis's ways, and that Otis was the only man Cinder let get close enough to touch her.

Cinder had her own ways. She was beautiful and known for

her copper-colored skin and that long black Indian hair. She kept to herself, kept back from folks like they weren't no good for her. Even when she would be standin right in front of you, she be lookin down or away, but then sometimes she turn her head, and real quick, and look at you with them black fiery eyes she has. You turn away, then all day long you remember her that way. Cinder walked gracefully, could walk like somethin she ain't never seen, walked like she was a ballet princess, could prance up on her toes, light with her steps, and then a sudden silence would follow her away.

Cinder was Alma's girl. Folks said she was just like her mama. Sam Turner had Alma livin up there with him behind Stony Mound, said she could live there with him and he be a good man for her, but Patch folks knew Alma was already carryin a baby when fore she went up there, and it sure wasn't gonna be none of that Sam Turner's child. Had to be that Grayson boy's, that one that was real tall and had that coal-black hair. Them Grayson boys always be comin across the creek and tryin to get them sassy Patch girls up to them fields. Them Grayson boys lived right over there on Dillion Street, just across the Catfish. Grayson boys wern't that bad, not as bad as them other Saturday-night white boys comin down from town all red-faced with that liquor in them.

Alma been dead for a while. Alma's sister Katey says all them other children that Sam Turner had Alma havin caused her dyin, broke her down, made her sick all the time, coughin and spittin herself up. Katey went on up there and got Cinder when Alma died. Katey sorta had somethin special for Cinder, bein so different from the others. Sam Turner wanted to keep Cinder, but Katey said, "Ya ain't keepin this child."

Cinder was still just a young thing when her mama died and Katey come and got her, she wasn't much past ten, al-

ready had hair down her back. Cinder was different. Sure,
you could look at her, speak and yell at her, but you could
not seem to touch her, she was different; come Sunday, down
at First Star Baptist, she sit in that church and wouldn't look
at anybody. She might hum, but never sing. Other girls her
age kept away from her, but the boys be sniffin at her skirts
like coon dogs. If one of them get too close, teased her at all,
she look at em with them eyes and stare em down to their
knees. Then she walk on, and whatever she was wearin would
sway with her walk, bring color and beauty to that coarse
bare dusty road out in front of that church.

A Mississippi summer night. Hot. Cinder was sixteen and
restless, leanin against the porch post. Them night bugs just
wouldn't leave her be, buzzin and bitin. She is not answerin
to the call of her name.

"Cinder, Cinder, child, ya hear me callin ya?" Katey calls.

Cinder's eyes stay in the night.

"Cinder, child, ya hear me callin ya?"

Cinder slowly turns her head but does not look beyond her
shoulder. Katey stands in the doorway, her face is strained,
she calls again, "Child, ya hear me?"

Cinder just don't answer, been bothered all day, pickin out
there in them pickin fields, yankin at things that ain't movin.
Field men hollerin and chantin all day like they do every day.
But Cinder is cool now, the summer night's soothin. She'd
washed and rinsed herself and just let the cool water stay and
glisten on her skin. She put that pale-yellow dress on, the one
she washed out and hung in the summer sun all day. Now it
clings to her, moves and sways with her.

"Cinder, ya hear me?"

"I'm just standin out here."

The night moves and Cinder moves into it, steppin softly

into the yard dirt. She can hear the sounds of her life behind her, Patch children cryin, mamas tryin to hush em, field men roarin at their women, porch-sitters laughin and talkin, tryin to outtalk the hollerin.

Cinder sneaks away and slithers into the dark. She is goin beyond the fences, down weavin paths to the old Patch Road, down the road some, away from them Patch shacks, past the smell of them summer outhouses, past the eyes of the porch-sitters, to where the Catfish flows. She turns from the road, feels the cool grass beneath her feet, climbs up that little grassy hill, then up some more to where the grass has grown higher, to where she sits now, pulls that pale-yellow dress far above her knees, lets that cool breeze from the creek blow on her legs. She knows he'll come, knows she'll make him come to her. He'll come through the dark, stand as she sits, then kneel when she won't look up at him. He'll kneel to her, whisper to her, then she'll look into his eyes. . . .

Cinder and a cold Mississippi night. Fires burn, smoke floats into the darkness. Cinder's screams shatter the silence. Pain comes to her and rips her soul apart, then leaves her twistin and squirmin. She keeps her eyes shut until it comes again. She does not look up into the dark sweaty faces lookin down at her, watchin her twist and shake beneath their eyes.

The other women are silent, but Katey pleads. "Child, don't fights it, don't fights it, let it come, let it come, Katey here wit ya, let it come, cry it out, child, cry it out." Katey closes her eyes, turns away from Cinder's pain, she whispers to herself and the other women that come at birthin time, "This child too tender for this, hurtin too much. Good Jesus, Good Jesus, Lord have mercy, Jesus."

A cold Mississippi night can be a slow night, fires burn long into the hours. The dark winds have carried Cinder's screams and cries. A softer cry has come, it too cries into the night as it cuddles on its mother's breast. Cinder has stilled herself, feels the warmth of her child on her breast. Her eyes are open, starin at this child, this part of her that's hers, will be of her ways. She can feel it and wants the warmth of its breathin on her breast. She sees no difference between the child and herself. The other women are smiling. Katey has given thanks to her Jesus. A gleeful voice ask, "What ya callin him?" Cinder's eyes are on the child, she is silent, then answers softly, "I'm gonna call him Billy Lee."

The night is gone.

Days came, same days, same hot suns and dusty roads. Same nights came again too, hot nights with folks hollerin and carryin on. But Otis was gone. He had come to Cinder, whispered to her, took her down in that deep grass by the Catfish, whispered to her soft whispers like the cool breeze comin from the Catfish, "Ya my woman, the only woman there ever be for me, Ah need ya, need ya wit me. Ah love ya, Cinder, love everything about ya. This here place ain't right for ya and me, gots ta gits someplace better, be someplace where they ain't got no pickin fields, someplace where they gots streetcars and picture shows, pretty dresses for ya. Ain't nothin down here for us. Ya too pretty for this old ugly place."

Otis had a strong look, but his look would weaken, his eyes would still. He couldn't take his eyes from Cinder's, couldn't stop his mind from thinkin about her, takin her wherever he was, takin her far away. "Ah love ya, Cinder. Ah goin ta Chicago and gits me one of them good-money jobs, gits me one of them shiny cars, then Ah comin back here and gits ya and takes ya away from here."

Otis wouldn't go to church, wouldn't stay in them pickin

fields at all. He'd fight just as quick as lightnin flash, had that wild-dog temper. Fight them Patch boys all the time. Went after one of them Saturday-night white boys one time, had Sheriff Tom comin down the Patch after him.

Otis was Sebella Owens' boy, but she could not do anything with him after his daddy died. His daddy would take him out behind one of them sheds and take a whippin stick to him, try and beat some of that temper out the boy, but folks say, after a while, Otis wouldn't even yell. Whippin just made him meaner. Sometimes you could feel him comin, didn't have to see him, could feel them eyes peerin at you, could see that tall slender body with that buckeye-brown shiny skin before you even turned around and made sure it was him. Otis could look you hard, had them kind of eyes that could make them rollin-dice stop on the dots, he wanted them to. Had them good looks and them quick ways, but that mad-dog temper got loose sometimes. Otis almost cut the life out that Elmer Brown, cut that boy up real bad just over talk. Otis left in the night, folks sorta figure he got on one of them night-rollin trains, probably to Chicago or Saint Louie, figure he ain't never comin back, but Cinder waits with Billy Lee.

Cinder took to herself even more after Billy Lee was born, kept that baby close to her all of the time, wouldn't let nobody touch him cept Katey. She knew the whispers and the talk, knew them porch-sitters were sayin things, porch-talkin about Otis. "That boy ain't never comin back for that girl. Leavin her wit that baby and no man ta care for em. Ain't right. Ah knew all along that Otis Owens up ta no good. He ain't comin back here. Wit them ways he gots, somebody done cut him ta death already."

Some days Cinder would just stand on that porch, lean against that porch post, stare with those eyes of hers, just be lookin far beyond where the sun drops, far past where her world ended, where thoughts could go no further, trains and folks disappear, but thoughts come smashing back. In the eves, Cinder would have that baby in her arms, ease her way through the chatter of porch-sitters, take her own paths she knows in the dark, sit in that tall grass down by the Catfish wit that child in her lap, look down in his eyes, smile at him, take her hand and touch his face. Cinder is whisperin now, her words flow slow and soft like the waters of the Catfish.

"Just look at you. Look how pretty you are. You're mama's pretty baby, ain't you? You gonna be big and strong just like your daddy, ain't you? Look at you, got your daddy's eyes, don't you? You like it down here, just with me. I know, Mama knows, all them folks up there make too much fuss for you, but Mama goin to keep her baby away from them, Mama goin to keep her baby happy, goin to love her baby. It's just you and me, Billy, then your daddy goin to come down that old Patch road one day, he gonna have one of them big cars, he goin to come and get us, take us back to Chicago, take us away from here, further than trains can go. Then it's goin' to be just me, you, and Daddy. We goin' to have a pretty house, gonna have a pretty yard with a garden, have some pretty flowers too, red ones, yellow ones. Mama loves you. Mama loves her Billy."

Cinder still watched for Otis and the days kept goin by, then the years came and they too went by. Billy Lee grew, was walkin and wantin to run, started showin some of his daddy's ways, until the Mississippi nights came, then he come to Cinder, curl under her warmth in the stills and chills of the nights.

Patch folks watched Cinder wait, then slowly turn with the time that no longer cared who waited on it. Cinder started goin down LeRoy's place, sippin on some of that corn liquor he made down there, then, if she felt like it, she'd dance. If she danced, she glowed like fire in the dark, curled into the desires of field men, then vanished into the night.

Ten years came, ten long slow times. Things ain't looked no different, Patch Road still dusty, Patch shacks still there, maybe leanin a little more. Things were no different, couldn't tell if they were, just like another wrinkle line on some old face, couldn't tell it from the other lines time left. Cinder still looked up the road sometime, still hoped Otis was comin, but it was only hope she seem to need, not Otis. Billy Lee was showin more of his father's ways. He was growin slender, but had that fast walk and fast moves. His quick ways seemed to give him some strength, add muscle to his slenderness. He was runnin around the Patch with the rest of those Patch boys, gettin into this and that, sneakin off too. Had that bad temper like his daddy, Katey couldn't do anything with him. Only Cinder could make him mind.

It was Saturday morning, August 21, 1937. Cinder had taken the time well, it had only polished her beauty. She sits on the porch steps, turns slowly as she hears the patter of quick-runnin feet behind her. She sees the blur of her son as he passes quickly into the dirt yard. "Billy Lee," she whispers once. Billy stops, turns to her, and comes.

"Where you goin? You eat everything on your plate?" Cinder asks softly and watches Billy's eyes as she waits for him to answer her.

"Mama, Mama, me and Gumpy just goin down bys the Catfish. Gumpy say some big old cats just layin wheres that big trees fall ins. He say he seen em. He say they bigger than the ones Mister Moody gits. Gumpy says he seen em. Me and Gumpy goin ta . . ."

Cinder speaks, Billy hushes. "You and Gumpy stay on this side of the Catfish, don't be over in town pickin at things. You stay near, you hear. Come here. You wash your face? Come here, let me see you."

Billy moves closer to his mother, her hand gently touches his face. She looks into his eyes and sees them twitchin. She says again, "Billy Lee, you stay on this side of the Catfish, and you be back here for suppertime." Cinder watches Billy run down through the weavin paths, she can still see him leapin over yard junk, and now he's gone.

"Hey, Gumpy. Hey, Gumpy. Hey, Gumpy," Billy is callin. Gumpy is comin down through his shack's path and sayin with short quick breaths, "Billy, what takin ya so long? Ah been waitin."

"Ah ain't takes no time, what's ya talkin about? Ah hads ta eat. Come on, let's go," Billy yells over his shoulder and darts further down the Patch path. Gumpy follows.

Gumpy could never catch Billy, never outrun him, even though Gumpy was the oldest of the two, bigger too. Gumpy could beat Billy up if he got real mad, he could get Billy down and keep him down, and he did a few times, fightin over a good wood stick, or that broken lantern they found by the tracks. But most of the time Gumpy would back off from Billy, it was better to let Billy be, better not to fight him at all, feel his teeth bitin in your skin, feel his fingers diggin into your eyes. Even when the fights were over, they weren't for Billy Lee. His burnin stares haunt you, make you feel you have a water snake next to you. Sometime Billy would get that little foldin knife out, that little foldin knife he stole off one of them boxes out behind Mister Hanner's store. Billy could get that knife out real quick, even when he and Gumpy were just playin.

Billy Lee and Gumpy had their own paths, own roads, never took the Patch Road, had their own byways over fences, through tall grass. To the crows' eyes, shadowy dark bodies zigzagged across open green fields, sometimes runnin and leapin, sometimes barely walkin through the moments of their time.

"Hey, Gumpy, Gumpy—look." Billy shoutin and pointin. Gumpy's eyes widen, his lips quickly curl into a smile. Billy still points and yells, "Ya see it? See it? Look, Gumpy, see it?" Gumpy is smilin now and lookin far beyond Billy's pointin finger, lookin to where the far greens of the field touch the far blues of the sky. He too sees the faint puffs of curly smoke floatin against the far sky.

"That's comin real fast," Gumpy is yelling. "Bet that's the Memphis Flyer comin, ain't be no old freight."

The crows see them run, field mice hear them comin. They run through thick bushes, splash through the waterlands, slip and slide in its mud, but they do not stop or slow, just yell to one another, "Come on. Come on. This way. Ah ain't goin thats way. Come on, come on, Gumpy, it's be comin." Bushes thicken, Billy scoots through, Gumpy follows, but jerks from sticky thorns, and then they are there. The rusty rails with the shiny tops glisten as far as the eye can see. Billy standin on the tracks holding his hands over his eyes to shield the morning sun rays. He's running again, yelling over his shoulder, "Come on, Gumpy." Gumpy yells ahead, "Let's stays here. We can sees it here." Billy's yells come trailing back, "Come on, Gumpy, let's sees it down there. Come on, we cans git across the trestle, sees it there."

Through the sweat rolling down in Billy's eyes he can see the distant puffs of white steamy smoke bellowing and the blurry round blackness beneath its wiggling. "It's comin, it's comin. Ah sees it. See it?" he yells back over his shoulder. His legs are moving faster and faster. Gumpy is yelling, "It's comin faster. Look, bet it's comin a hundred."

"Up here, Gumpy. Let's git up here, we can sees it up here good, come on." Billy darts from the tracks and into the bushes, then climbs up through the tick weeds and stands on the top of a little grassy hill looking out over the murky grays and greenish blues of the waterland. The old brown log trestle stretching across shimmers in the sunlight. Billy can hear the train coming, the distant sneezing of its engine teases the air. Billy's eyes widen, Gumpy comes to his side with breath still panting, he yells, "Bet it comin faster than a bird can fly. Bet nothin can stop it, bets it be in Memphis fore a minute."

The old log trestle begins to shake and sway. The black round face of the engine snorts across the trembling trestle. Billy's and Gumpy's yells become smothered by the thunderous sound of the coming train. All their hearts can feel is the pounding of the world beneath their feet.

The big black-faced engine is passing, a burning wind is sizzling the air. Quick flashes of train men are seen, their gray train caps on, red and blue handkerchiefs around their necks, white reddish faces, ride through misty thick steam. The riding cars are passing, dark reds with long stripes of yellow letters on them streak by with shaded white faces looking out their windows, seeing the easy flow of the swamplands with its satin-still waters, seeing a quick blur of a grassy hillside where two little nigger boys stand.

The train is gone but the ground still quivers, the air's still hot and steamy from the fiery engine, only its trailing smoke

can be seen. Billy and Gumpy can hear themselves again,
they had to yell as the train sped by, but now they can hear
themselves. "Bet it's in town." "Bet it's past town." "Bet it be
ta Memphis fore we can counts ta ten."

Billy leaping down from the grassy mound and into the
thick bushes. Gumpy still stands on the little grassy hill and
lazily calls out, "Where's ya goin now? Hey, Billy, where's ya
goin, huh?" It is quiet on top of the little grassy hill, the
echoes of the train melted into the silence of the greens and
browns and satins of the waterlands. Gumpy waits in the silence, then yells again, "Where's ya goin, Billy Lee? Where's
ya goin? Ah stayin here, ain't crossin that. Ah ain't goin over
that. Ah ain't crossin that train bridge wit ya."

Billy moves quickly, takes quick steps, but carefully places
each foot down on the railroad ties of the tracks. His steps
are swift, but his stare is steady and slow, he watches
each step, peers down through the deep browns of the rail
ties, sees the mucky waters far below. He stills his quick
steps, centers his balance, shouts over his shoulder, "Gumpy,
come on, let's go over. Come on, hurry fore one of them old
freights be comin. Come on, Gumpy. Ya scared? Ya scared of
everything."

Gumpy stands in the stillness, watches Billy get further
and further across the trestle, higher and higher above the
swampy water where the water snakes live. Finally he moves
and the tracks come before him. Gumpy's steps slow; he
places his foot on the deep-brown rail ties, sees the mucky
waters beneath, another step follows slowly. "Come on,
Gumpy. Hurry up. Come on fore a freight be comin." Gumpy
hears Billy's calls, and tries to quicken his steps, then stops,
stills his balance, turns slowly, looks back. He has not come
that far, but far enough to feel the quivers in his chest. He

turns again slowly, looks afar to where Billy quickly steps above the water-snake waters, then moves slowly again. Billy stops, turns around on the tracks, and yells again, "Hurry up, Gumpy. Hurry up fore a train come."

Gumpy's steps quicken; without looking back, he can see the big black face of a freight train coming, feel it bearing down on him, see its big iron wheels rolling over him, cutting him in hafe. He can see hisself falling into the waters below, see all them water snakes curling, wiggling, then coming to get him. He turns his head, glances over his shoulder, sees the long quiet tracks behind him, but in his mind it's that big black ugly face of the train is coming, he turns and quickens his steps.

The crows had flew, the waters had rippled, the water snakes might have wiggled, but time had stilled for Gumpy. And then it was alive again. "Hey, Billy, wait up, wait up," he yells ahead. Billy slows his stride and they both walk side by side along the tracks that are far beyond the trestle. The miles and hours pass slowly, the moving sun is high, making their shadows shrink beneath their feet. The trees along the tracks have thickened into forest, the air is cooler, and the songbirds sing, but always at a distance.

"Hey, Gumpy, let's go down there."

Billy stills his walk and points to the shadowy path that leads from the tracks and into the shade of the trees. Gumpy watches Billy dart down the path, then he follows. The path curves through the trees, sometimes Billy can be seen, then sometimes he vanishes as the path twists and turns through the shade of the trees. "Hey, Gumpy, look over there. See? See it?" Gumpy's eyes widen as he looks through the trees and bushes.

The distant pondwater sparkles through the silent shade of

the trees. Gumpy shouts, "Ah ain't goin down there, Billy Lee. Ah ain't goin down there. We can'ts go down there, that's where them redhead boys be, we can'ts be goin down there. They chase us, they's big. Ah ain't goin down there. Ya knows what theys do before, ya remembers. They almost git us. Theys can beat us up bad if theys git us." Billy sighs, but still looks through the trees and bushes to the quiet waters of the pond. He turns and whispers to Gumpy, "Theys ain't be down there. Theys ain't goin ta see us. Come on, Gumpy, let's go. Ah ain't scared. Ah goes first. Come on wit me." Billy keeps his eyes on Gumpy's eyes, but they don't move. Gumpy just stares at the pond. Billy quickly whispers, "Ya scared. Ya be scared of everythings, ya more scared than an old lady be. Ya scared all the time of everything."

"Ah ain't be scared," Gumpy yells back.

2

Banes had its back-land folks, them folks that lived out past the waterland. Red Pasko lived out there on that Pasko land with his wife, Ginger, and his four boys and daughter. He stayed out there most of the time, worked his own fields, made his own way, except Saturdays. Come Saturdays, he come into town to get some store-bought goods and some good man-talk from other Banes men who liked to take their Saturdays with a little whiskey.

Banes men remembered Red Pasko from his younger days, him taking off and joining the Army and fighting over there in France against them Germans in the big war. He's been walking with that limp ever since, never said how he got it. He turned a little mean after he come home, but still liked his whiskey and some good talk.

Lori Pasko just turned fifteen, but still had her baby face with its crystal-blue eyes. She was still running barefoot in the summer, and when she ran, her long reddish hair flung from her like a flame of fire. She was a tough little girl, had that mean streak of her daddy and the quick-talking way of her mother, which helped her get in them schoolyard fights of hers. At home she had her brothers, two older and two younger. David, the oldest, was the only one could still outrun her, catch her, hold her down, tickle and tease her; then, when he let her up, he knew he better run. Her daddy would take a stick to those boys in a minute, but, as mean as he could get, he never lay a hand on Lori.

Ginger Pasko could yell up a storm and keep them boys in line, could keep Lori reminded she was a girl and a Pasko. Not too many other folks lived out that way, which was fine with the Paskos. The Currans lived out there, but they weren't nothing but Paskos too, you could tell they were kin, with that same red hair. Paskos didn't bother anybody and made it clear that they didn't want to be bothered at all.

Summertime, hot days, but there was always a little shade and a place where secrets could be told. It was Cousin Jenny that Lori would tell her secrets to, talk about days gone by, days coming, things they might have to sneak and do. Then, sooner or later, Jimmy Tignor or Nathan Bradley's name would pop up, them boys at school that Lori would not look at. Down over the hill from the fields and far from the house is where the big fat oak sits, that's where secrets are told, where boyfolks and mothers won't be trying to get in their business.

Neither Lori or her cousin Jenny, who wasn't much different than Lori and only a year younger, would ever wear a dress, unless it was Sunday and down at the Baptist church

and their mamas made them. They felt better in them boys'
pants, especially them ones be fitting a little tight. They
could both sneak some words and use them too, words they
hear them boys using and some of them words their daddies
might use when they were all red-faced and swaying with
that Saturday-night liquor. Lori could sneak some of them
store-bought cigarettes, them Lucky Strikes kind her daddy
would get.

"What's wrong with you?" Jenny throws her head back to
get the hair out of her eyes and then ask Lori again, "What's
wrong with you? You ain't said nothin since you come out.
What's ailing you now, huh?" Lori begins to pout, curls her
lip up, and says, "Mama been yellin all damn mornin. You
know how she gets, every damn mornin she starts."

Lori is making faces and flinging her hands in the air as
she is saying, "Every time I turn around she starts, Do this,
do that, did you do this?, did you do that?, ain't you done
this?, ain't you done that? She's probably still up there yellin
and carryin on. I'll be glad when I'm old enough to get out of
here, go up to Memphis, just get away from here."

"Oh, hush," Jenny says, "your daddy ain't lettin you go to
no Memphis. He'd have a fit and you know it."

"Watch me," Lori shouts, "you just watch me, you hear."

Lori kept on about Memphis and what she was going to do
until Jenny busted in, asking, "You get any cigarettes? Give
me one." Lori's still pouting, reaches down in her boy-shirt
pocket, and gets a cigarette, then slows her words, jerks her
head back, and says, "I just got a few. I'm goin to light it."

"Let me light it."

"No." Lori shakes her head. "I'm goin to light it, and if
you don't hush, I ain't givin you none. I got the damn things,
you didn't."

The little red tip of the match scrapes against the side of the matchbox, then burst into a little yellow flame. Lori waits until the flame settles before she slowly brings the match up to the cigarette she has hold of with her lips. She squints her eyes and sucks on the cigarette till she taste the smoke, then flicks the match away and sucks again till she has a mouthful of smoke. She turns to her cousin and, without changing the expression she has on her face, blows the smoke in Jenny's face. Jenny shouts, "You asshole, you're an asshole, Lori."

Now Jenny is whispering, "Nathan likes you and you like Nathan, don't you? You just don't want nobody knowin. You like him, don't you, Lori? Just say it."

Lori takes another deep drag on the cigarette, holds the smoke in her mouth, then blows it out slowly and likes the light dizzy feeling she is getting. "Nathan Bradley," she is saying, "can kiss my ass."

"Ah, he's cute," Jenny yells, "Nathan's cute."

"He ain't nothin but a skinny mama's boy, that's all he is," Lori yells back. "He ain't cute. You think he's so cute, then you get him, you can nurse him too." Lori smiles before saying, "You probably like nursin him, anyway." Jenny starts fussin. "Nathan's just as cute as Jimmy Tignor. He's just as cute." Lori starts shaking her head and flinging her hands at Jenny. "Jimmy Tignor, Jimmy Tignor," she's shouting, "Jimmy Tignor this, and Jimmy Tignor that. That's all you talk about, Jimmy Tignor, Jimmy Tignor. Ain't a boy around here wort horse. Jimmy Tignor can kiss my ass too."

Jimmy Tignor came and went, so did Nathan Bradley and talk of Memphis, but the shade and the secret world beneath the big oak tree stayed. Lori laid down in the tall grass, while Jenny leaned back against the fat oak's belly. They were both comfortable in their silence until Jenny asked, "You think David is going to marry Kathy? You think he's asked her yet? She probably wants him to."

Lori reached and got another cigarette and lit it, then watched the smoke float up through the tall grass and make its own little clouds above her head. She thinks of her brother David, can see his image coming into the smoke, can see his rough ways, his cussin all the time, Mama yellin at him, and that Kathy Weaver with them wimpy ways always big-eyein him, looking like she's ready to cry all the time. "He ain't marryin her. She's too ugly for David to be marryin." Lori shouts, then pouts, "She is seventeen already and her boobs ain't as big as mine yet. She goin to be flat-chested just like some old bare wall. Besides, David'd drive her crazy. He ain't ready for no wife, especially her. Havin kids lookin like comic-book pictures. He's just doin it to her, probably. I see him sneakin out, goin that way, then sneakin back like he ain't been nowhere."

Jenny was a pretty girl. Although a year younger than Lori, she was a little taller, had slender ways about her, had a way of smiling with her eyes as she did when she heard Lori saying, "Jenny, if I tell you something, you swear not to tell nobody, ever?" Jenny sits up, scoots closer to Lori, and whispers, "What, Lori?" "You got to swear first. You got to swear before I tell you," Lori demands. Jenny whispers, "I ain't goin to tell nobody. I won't tell, I promise." Then she jerks her head and looks away.

"Lori, Lori," Jenny whispers sharply, tugs at Lori's leg, and whispers again, "Lori, Lori, look down at the pond. Look, someone coming. Look, see?" Lori sits up and brushes the hair from her eyes, then looks down through the tall grass to where she can see the bluish-green waters of the pond. She looks for a moment, then says to Jenny, "Girl, ain't nobody over there."

"Them niggers." Jenny's whisper almost burst into a yell, she points, lowers her voice, saying, "See, see comin in them bushes, see em? See em now, see em?" Lori's eyes widen, she can see the shadowy colored heads and arms wiggling through the green bushes on the other side of the pond. She blurts out, "Shit, what they doin down there?," then stills herself and watches the dark figures come into the clearing of the pond.

"Them just two little boys," Jenny says, sighing. Lori's face tightens, she whispers harshly, "I don't want them around here. That's my pond and I don't want their nigger asses in it." Jenny smiles and whispers to Lori, "Ya want to chase em?" Lori has a bigger smile on her face as she leans towards Jenny and whispers in her ear, "Let's sneak up and catch em, you want to do that? We can sneak around and get in them trees, then come in the bushes behind em, then we can get em."

Lori had hunted with her brothers, snuck around and chased rabbits their way, followed them after coon and fox, kept up with them too. She could sit as still as a stone, just waiting till that squirrel'd stick his head around that tree trunk. She tiptoes through the bushes and small trees. From time to time, she stops and listens to the sounds coming from the pond, then sneaks on. Jenny follows, but not as quiet. "Shish, shish. You want to scare em away? Shish," Lori whispers. The splashing sounds and boyish shouts are louder now. Lori is crouched and peering through the bushes. Jenny creeps up behind her. "What ya gonna do with em when we catch em?" she ask. "Hush," Lori whispers over her shoulder, then hisses, "Look at em, look at em. Got their nigger asses in my pond. Just wait till I catch em."

Billy had darted from the bushes and ran towards the pond. "Come on, Gumpy, come on. Ya still scared? Ain't nobody's here, see. What ya scared for? Theys come, theys can'ts catch us. We can runs back the ways we came. Ya chicken, ya still be afraid." Billy yells back to Gumpy, then scampers up to the water's edge. The pondwaters ripple gently, although they seem still, not moving at all in the center. The thick bushes and low-hanging branches of trees reflect their vibrant colors in the still waters.

Gumpy sneaks out of the bushes, takes a few steps, and looks around, then walks slowly up to where Billy stands peering into the water. "Ya see anything in there, see any redbacks?" Gumpy ask at a near whisper. "Naw, not yet," Billy shouts, "but Ah bet there be some in there. Ah bet there be some big ones just a layin in there. Theys might be out there in the middles, be out there under them lilies." Billy picks up a stick and starts poking into the water. Gumpy lifts his head and lets his eyes roll around the bushes on the far side of the pond.

"What ya doin?" Gumpy blurts out. Billy's rolling up his pants leg and yells back to Gumpy, "Its ain't deep. See, ya can see the bottom. See, its ain't deep. Ah goin in somes." Billy steps into the pond, the mud squishes between his toes, he takes more mushy steps. He pokes his stick into the depths of the pond, watches the muddy bottom of the pond ooze into a murky mist, then yells back over his shoulder, "Hey, Gumpy, come on. It ain't deep, see, Ah tells ya, it ain't deep. Come on."

Gumpy wades into the pond, stops and looks around, then

wades further into the water. His head jerks around, he shouts back over his shoulder, "Billy, Billy, Ah hear somin. Ya hear it? Somin comin." Billy turns, looks around, then yells back to Gumpy, "Ya ain't hears nothin. Ain't nothin be there. Ya still scared." Gumpy jerks his head around again. Billy jerks too and yells, "Run, Gumpy, run, Gumpy."

The waters of the pond splash and surge, ripples are thrust into waves. Billy and Gumpy dash through the water.

"Ya niggers get out of there. Get out of there. Ya hear me? God damn ya," Lori shouts. She'd stalked like a cat, almost crawled through the bushes, but now she has sprung, moves with leaps along the water's edge, yelling, "I'm goin to kick the shit out of ya all."

Billy's eyes widen, jerk back and forth from the redheaded white faces running at him to the muddy bank of the far end of the pond that he's racing to. He must get there before that screaming white girl; he runs, falls into the mucky water, gets back up. His feet slip and slide, he falls again, and again, but gets back up. He can see the fiery hair and sneering face coming at him, reaching for him.

Jenny follows Lori's leaps and yells, watches the two little niggers slipping and splashing frantically through the water, watches Lori reaching for the skinny one that's jerking away from her reach, then she sees Lori yank the nigger and pull him down under her and climb on his back while he still tries to crawl away.

"Ya little black-ass son of a bitch," Lori yells as she rides Billy back down into the mud.

Billy's face is shoved down in the mud, but he is jerking and squirming like a catfish out of water. Sharp nails dig and claw at his back and arms. He jerks upwards, but Lori rides him back down to his knees, then crushes him down to the ground.

"Get that one, get em," Lori yells to Jenny as she pushes Billy further beneath her.

Jenny turns and sees the other nigger rushing for the bank. She runs towards him, grabs at his arms. "Come mere, come mere, ya asshole," she yells as she reaches for Gumpy.

Gumpy's eyes glare white with fear, his arm is being yanked at, clawed at. He turns and twists until he is free. Jenny yells, "Ya asshole, asshole." Then he is grabbed again. Both of Jenny's hands are pulling and yanking at his arms, jerking him around. He swings around, smashes his fist into Jenny's face, then springs into the bushes.

"Lay still. Ya hear me, I said lay still, nigger," Lori shouts and smacks the back of Billy's neck. "Shit," she yells as Billy lunges and squirms beneath her. She climbs higher on his back and grabs at his outstretched arms. "Shit, ya son of a bitch," she yells again and smashes her butt down onto Billy's skinny back.

"Git off me. Git off me, girl. Git off me," Billy screams, then twist his head around, opens his mouth, and bites into Lori's arm.

"Ya son of a bitch, ya nigger fuckin bastard. I'll beat the shit out of ya, ya hear me?" Lori screams, grabs Billy around his neck and jerks his head back, then digs her fingers into his face.

Billy stills to a quiver. His head is being pushed down into the mud and held. Lori sits high on his back and yells to Jenny, "Where's that other one, ya get him?" Jenny shouts back, "I couldn't get him, he hit me in the face, then run off in the bushes." Jenny comes closer, she has her hand on the side of her face, her eyes stare down at Billy. She starts kicking at his arms and head, screaming, "Look what ya all did, you hit my face, you little bastard, you asshole."

"This one didn't get away. This one didn't get away, did ya, nigger? Did ya?" Lori yells and wiggles her butt down harder on Billy's back, then yells, "Get his arms, Jenny, get that arm. Flip him over. Hold his arms still so I can flip him over."

Billy's arms are being jerked and pulled, his shoulders are being shook and yanked. He closes his eyes tightly as he is flipped over on his back, then groans when Lori's weight comes crashing down on his chest. "Look what I got," Lori taunts and scoots higher on Billy's chest, then gets his arms pinned under her knees. "Look what I got, look what I got," Lori taunts, then slaps Billy's face.

Billy's eyes flash open and glare up into the white face with the fiery hair that looks down at him. "Git off me, git off me, girl," Billy shouts and twists.

Lori wiggles her butt down on Billy's chest and taunts, "Ya ain't goin nowhere, ya hear me? Ya ain't goin nowhere," then spits down in Billy's face.

Billy's eyes glow red, his nostrils flare. Lori screams, "What ya lookin at, huh?," then scoots higher up on Billy's chest, pushes her knees down harder into his shoulders, and with both hands starts beating and clawing at his face.

Jenny smiles and watches, then yells, "Lori, let him go. Let him go, he's crying, let him go."

Billy's wiggles, jerks, and lunges have stilled. Tears run from his glaring eyes, blood bubbles from the scratches on his face.

Lori sits with ease on his chest. "What's wrong, ya a little mama's boy? Ya a little mama's boy, huh?" Lori taunts at Billy's face. Then slowly she leans forward on her knees, lets her weight push Billy's shoulders further beneath her, then she stands with her hands on her hips and looks down at the face at her feet. "Get out of here. Ya better get, fore I change my mind."

Billy turns over on his stomach, pushes hisself up with his hands, then stands staring into Lori's eyes before he turns and slowly begins to walk away. He brings his hand to his pocket and slides it in. His fingers grab at the slippery pocket knife, then he slides his hand out of his pocket and brings it up in front of him. He slowly brings his other hand up to where he holds the folding knife and begins to pluck at it with his fingers until the blade pops out of the handle.

"Ya better get out of here. Ya better run, fore I come get ya again. Ya hear me?" Lori shouts at Billy as she only sees the skinny boy just walking away.

Billy moves slowly, he does not run.

"Damn ya," Lori yells and runs up behind him, pushing at his back.

Billy snarls over his shoulder, "Ya better leave me be's, Ah kills ya, Ah kills ya."

"God damn ya, nigger," Lori shouts, grabs Billy's back, and yanks him around.

Billy turns with Lori's yank, his right hand lunges at her, the knife blade plunges into her ribs. She gasps for air. Billy pulls the knife out and lashes with it again, the blade slices into Lori's arm. Her mouth flies open, she screams, but only low moans come. She grabs her side, turns from Billy and begins to stagger, her legs are quivering, her arms are twitching, her hands shake and fill with blood.

"Ah tells ya, Ah tells ya, girl," Billy shouts, then runs into the bushes and away from the screams that come.

"Lori, Lori, oh God, Lori. Lori. Lori," Jenny screams and

cries, her eyes cannot turn or blink from the blood she sees.

Lori is falling, her legs wobble, she falls to the ground and moans, slowly turns herself over, and lays gasping.

Jenny comes to her side, kneels, and looks into Lori's trembling face. "Lori, Lori, God, Lori, Lori." Now Jenny jerks herself up, turns, and runs from the pond, up through the bushes, through the tall grass, past the fat oak tree, up the hill and into the fields, screaming, "Lori's hurt, she's bleedin. Lori, Lori. Aunt Ginger, Aunt Ginger. Help, help, David, David, Aunt Ginger."

Ginger Pasko is annoyed by the dogs barking, she moves away from the cooking stove and looks out the window. She wipes her hands on her apron and sighs, thinking it is too early for her husband to be coming home. She peers through the window, then walks to the screen door and looks down the red dirt road that leads to the house. She shrugs and starts to yell at the barking dogs.

David and Kevin Pasko are in the yard behind the barn. David has also heard the dogs barking and comes to the fence, peeks over, then yells, "Shut up. Shut that barkin up." The dogs whine, then bark again.

Ginger Pasko begins to turn back to the cooking stove, then hears screams and runs out onto the porch. Jenny is running and screaming across the fields. Ginger Pasko yells for her son, "David, David."

The howls and barks of the Pasko dogs pierce into the hot sticky air. They pull at their ropes and chains.

"Come on, Kevin," David yells, jumps over the fence, and breaks into a run across the barnyard and then into the fields. "Jenny, Jenny, what's wrong?" he yells.

Jenny's run slows to a stagger, she begins to stumble and fall, then gets back up again, running and screaming, "Lori, Lori, Lori's bleedin, Lori's hurt, she's bleedin."

Ginger Pasko can see Jenny stumbling and waving her hands in the far field. She snatches her apron off, runs off the porch, and starts running across the field, yelling, "Jenny, where's Lori? What happened? Where's Lori, where's Lori?"

David has reached Jenny, takes her into his hands, holds her gently and asks, "What's wrong? What happen, Jenny? Where's Lori at?" Jenny jerks her head over her shoulder, tears fling from her eyes, she screams, "She bleedin, she's bleedin down the by pond, she's hurt, David, she's hurt bad. That nigger stuck her with somin."

David runs for the pond, his heart pounds across the field, down the hill, past the fat oak, into the high grass, and down through the bushes. He is yelling, "Lori, where are you? Lori, Lori." He sees her lying on the other side of the pond and runs around the muddy bank, then dives to his knees as he reaches her side. He looks at her face, touches it, then looks at the blood soaking her shirt and flowing through her hands. "Oh my God," he gasps. He reaches for her hand and gently pulls it from her chest. When he touches her he can feel her tremble and shake. He hears her moaning, "Mommy, Mommy . . ." He whispers to her, "It's David, I'm here, Lori. Just lay still." He moves her hand, opens her shirt, and pulls it away from her skin. Blood is squirting from the hole beneath her breast. He reaches for his handkerchief, then gently begins to pat at the wound, but the blood still comes. He gently lifts her into his arms, but carries her as fast as he can and whispers down into her ear, "I got ya, Lori, I got ya, you be all right. We'll be home soon, Mama can fix it, don't cry, Lori, Mama can make it better."

Kevin has neared and is shouting, asking what happen, will Lori be all right, but David only says, "Kevin, do as I say, go get the truck, go into town, get Doc Grey. Tell him Lori's knife-stabbed, then find Daddy, tell him some nigger knifed Lori. Go, Kevin, for God sake hurry."

David reaches the top of the hill and can quicken his steps on the level field. His mother's screams have reached him. She is running to him, he yells to her, "She's alive, Mama, she's still alive."

Lori's mother's hands can touch her now, she rubs the hair from Lori's face and looks into her eyes as she gently pulls the bloody shirt from her side and lifts the handkerchief from her skin. "Hurry, David, get her into the house," Ginger Pasko quickly says, then whispers, "Baby, baby, it's Mama, Mama's here."

The dogs are barking furiously, their howls shriek through the air, birds flutter for the sky. Jenny sits on the porch steps crying. The younger boys have come to her, they sit beside Jenny and begin to cry as they watch their big brother carrying Lori up the steps and into the house. They saw the blood and their mother's tears.

David lays his sister on his mother's bed, then gently takes her legs and eases them so that Lori lays comfortably. His mother shouts, "David, get that white pan from under the sink, get some water, and get some clean sheets, hurry."

David runs from the room. It is quiet, and Ginger Pasko can hear her daughter's short, gasping breath. She leans over Lori and rubs the hair from her face, looks into her eyes, then quickly looks back at the bloody wound. She dabs the blood away with the already soaked handkerchief. She is thinking the wound does not look bad, but she has to get the bleeding stopped. Again she reaches for Lori's face and rubs her cheek, then whispers, "Baby, baby, Mama's here, you're gonna be just fine, honey. . . ."

Lori's eyes twitch, her lips are quivering, she's trying to talk, but can only gasp, "Mommy, it hurts . . . it hurts. . . ."

Time is no friend, it has turned its back and will not help, will not move anything, will not slow things down that are moving. It will not stop the blood seeping from Lori's side, it will not bring Doctor Grey up the road. It will not be intimidated by the curses hissed at it, nor will it show mercy for Ginger Pasko's pleads that beg it to give, pray for it not to take. Where it has given hours, days, years, it will not yield moments. Where it has given moments so freely and with abundances, it now gives eternity.

Lori is dead.

Doctor Henry P. Grey hurries out of his car, grabs his black leather bag, wipes the sweat from the back of his neck, and rushes up the steps. He looks at the faces of the children sitting on the porch as he hurries by them and into the house, then into the room where Ginger Pasko sits holding the limp body of her daughter in her arms. He sighs, then slows his steps towards her.

"She's just sleepin, she's just asleep, she was tired," Ginger Pasko whispers up to Doc Grey.

"I know, Ginger, I know, I know," Doc Grey whispers, then gently says, "Let me take her now, Ginger. Let Doc Grey have Lori now. Let me see her, Ginger. Let me take care of her now. You go on out on the porch and see to them children. I'll take care of Lori now." He takes Lori into his arms and gently lays her back down on the bed, then waits until her mother walks slowly out of the room, then closes the door.

Sheriff Tom's dusty black Ford comes flying up the road, he jumps out the car and runs up the porch, looks around at the still faces, mumbles, "Doc Grey inside here?," then goes barreling into the house. He taps on the closed door, whispers harshly, "Doc Grey, Sheriff Tom here," then goes into the room. He looks at the blood-covered bed, the lifeless face, then lowers his head and slowly shakes it back and forth. "My God, Henry, what done happened to this child here?"

Doc Grey turns towards the sheriff, sighs, and lets his words drift out slowly. "By the time I got out here, she was gone. Don't think I could have done much anyway, from the looks of things. Someone shoved a blade right up between her ribs, just far enough to nip at her heart. That's about all I can tell now. Of course, I'll be making a report and all. I'm just trying to get her a little presentable, get her cleaned up some for her kin. She got another slash on her arm. Looks like she may have tried to fight it off some, then looks like that second stab just got in at the right spot. We ain't had nothin like this in a long while."

The sheriff walks closer to the bed, looks quickly at Lori from head to toe, then ask Doc Grey, "Henry, was she bothered any?"

"I don't think she's been bothered, Tom. I haven't checked thoroughly yet, but her coveralls were buttoned up pretty tight, don't look like nobody was yankin on them. Of course, I can let you know for sure. The only thing I noticed, on her right arm, right up from her wrist a bit, looks like some bite marks, looks like she put up a pretty good fight." Doc Grey let his words drift off, then went back to getting the blood off Lori.

Sheriff Tom went out and stood on the porch, but kept his distance for a moment. David had his mother in his arms, both of them sat trembling. The younger boys still sat beside Jenny, the tears were still falling from all their eyes. Sheriff

Tom made a grunting sound, cleared his throat, then seemed to twist his thick neck a little and walked over to David and his mother and knelt down, cleared his throat again, and whispered the best he could, "David, I got to know what happened here. You think you can tell me?"

"Nigger did it, Sheriff, nigger did it down at the pond. We were up here. Jenny come runnin across the field, just a screamin." David's words are becoming slurred, but he blurts out clearly, "My sister's dead, and that nigger goin to pay for it."

The sheriff stood, took a little time to wipe the sweat from the back of his neck, looked down at David and his mother, and mumbled, "Son, you just take care of your mama now. I promise you, I'll have this nigger fore that sun goes down."

Sheriff Tom walks over to Jenny, looks down at her, looks at the other children. The youngest boy looks up with a small smile on his face, but stays quiet. The sheriff reaches down and pats the boy's head, then kneels in front of Jenny's blank stare. Her eyes blink, then she lifts her head and stares over Sheriff Tom's shoulder.

"You're Jenny, arn't ya?" the sheriff ask, sighs, and waits for Jenny to look at him. She doesn't. Sheriff Tom takes a deep breath, then says, "Jenny, I'm goin to tell you something, and I'm goin to want you to listen to Sheriff Tom here, and then you and me, we're goin to walk over to that barn fence, and just me and you goin to talk for a while, nobody else, just you and me, honey. But first I want you to listen to what I'm goin to tell you: Ain't nobody goin to hurt ya ever again. Sheriff Tom here tellin ya that. Now I want you to take your hand and put it in mine, come now, just let Sheriff Tom take your hand. That's it, sugar, that's a girl. Come on to Sheriff Tom, that's a girl."

The sheriff stands. Jenny has his hand and slowly begins to rise. When she does, he pulls her close to him and puts his arm over her shoulder. She leans against him as they walk towards the barn fence and then the bench by the barn door. They sit, but Jenny still leans against him. He doesn't say anything, just sits and pats her shoulder. Jenny begins to cry again. The sheriff is quiet, just pats her shoulder and rocks and sways with her.

The dogs have quieted, quit their barking and howling, but they whine. The birds soar gracefully over the fields, some landing, picking at things, then just flying away again. Sheriff Tom did not see the birds, the blur of Lori's blood was still in his eyes. He sighs as he keeps patting Jenny's shoulder, then softly ask, "Honey, who put them scratches on your face? Tell Sheriff Tom who did that to you. Was it that nigger that hurt Lori?"

Jenny shakes her head no.

"Who did that to you, then?" the sheriff asks.

"That other one," Jenny answers.

"Two of em, you say two of em came down there?"

"That's all Ah seen."

"You ever seen these niggers before?"

"Ah ain't never seen em around here."

"That one that scratched you, did that to your face, what he look like?"

"Ah ain't never seen him before. He was one of them dark kind, ain't had no hair."

"You mean he was old, had a bald head?"

"No, he was just a boy, he wasn't real old."

"You say he was just a boy?"

"He was bigger than the other one, but he wasn't old."

"That one that hurt Lori, was he just a boy?"   .

"He was a little skinny nigger."

"How old you think they might be?"

"Ah don't know, Ah don't know. Ah ain't sure."

"You thinkin they might be fifteen . . . sixteen . . . maybe even twenty?"

"They wern't that old yet, they were little niggers."

"You thinkin they maybe . . . twelve . . . thirteen . . . about that?"

"Maybe."

"You think you might know em if you see em again?"

"That one that knifed Lori, I'd know him for sure."

"What they have on, you remember? What were they wearin?"

"Ah don't know, just shirts and pants, Ah guess."

"That one that hurt you, what did he do to you?"

"Ah was chasin him, and he hit me in the face."

"You chased him, did he have a knife?"

"I chased him, he ran all up in them bushes, then he hit me and ran away."

"Did he have a knife too?"

"Ah ain't seen one."

"Did the other one beat on Lori?"

"No, she beat him up, then let him go."

"She beat him up, you say?"

"She got him good. He started cryin and all, she let him up."

"What happen then, tell Sheriff Tom, what happened then?"

"He . . ."

"Is that when he got that knife out and hurt Lori?"

"Uh huh."

The dogs started barking and howling again. The old battered blue pickup truck came roaring up the dirt path, leaving that red dirt trailing behind it like a dirty red wind. Ginger Pasko pushes away from David's arms and starts running to the truck. The truck stops and slides through the dirt, its door flies open, and Red Pasko scrambles out, dragging his limp leg. Quickly he stills hisself, looks around, pushes his wife aside as she reaches for him.

"Where is she, where's Lori?" Red Pasko shouts, hops up the porch steps, yanks the screen door open, and burst through the doorway, his wife's screams trail behind him.

Doctor Henry P. Grey had cleaned most of the blood off Lori, taken the bloody sheets and put them in a corner, made sure they were out of sight. Then he'd removed her shirt, folded it up tightly, and put it into his bag. He found one of Ginger's blouses that buttoned up the back and put Lori's limp arms through the sleeves, then folded her hands beneath her breast. He looked at her babylike face, shook his head, then reached out with his hand, gently closed her eyes, and pulled the blanket over her head. He would sit with her, that he could do for her.

Doctor Grey is up now, he has heard the shouts and the screams, and now he hears the uneven thump of someone rumbling into the house. He opens the bedroom door for Red Pasko, looks into his face until he catches his eyes with his own, then he leaves Lori with her father and slowly walks through the house, out onto the sitting porch.

The midafternoon sun glares, the blue sky seems to simmer. The porch is silent, except for soft sobbing, it is silent. Sheriff Tom has brought Jenny back to the porch and sat her with the younger ones. Now he leans against the porch post, his arms folded and resting above his massive belly. Ginger Pasko is motionless, she sits with her elbows on her legs and her face buried in her hands. David is with her. Kevin has come to the porch and sits with his cousin Jenny. He is silent. Doctor Grey is old, seen his years, the wrinkles in his face seem to catch the shadows of the sunlight baking down on it. He had glanced at Sheriff Tom, but they had not spoke, it was a time of keeping words.

Now the dogs bark, Sheriff Tom and Doc Grey keep still, the younger children turn and look towards the house as the crashing sounds of glass being broken and things smashing into walls shatter the silence. The screen door flies open and Red Pasko comes storming out onto the porch, then stops at its edge, throws his hands above his head, and shakes before he screams.

"Who did this? Who did this to my little girl, who did this?" Red Pasko's screams cannot carry his grief, and they break into cries of, "She's dead, my God, she's dead. Who did this, Tom? Ah want to know who did this to her? My God, somebody tell me who did this."

Sheriff Tom raises his head, sighs, and walks slowly up to Red Pasko. "Red, we got some talkin to do here, but not a lot of time for it. I talked to Jenny over there. She's all right, she's just hurtin real bad inside, seen too much for a day. You had some niggers comin in at your pond down there. From what I can tell, they were young uns . . . thirteen . . . fourteen maybe. Girls here try to chase em out of there, one of em pulls that knife. Now, I ain't sure if they're some of our niggers or some of them rail-driftin niggers just wanderin. But I know they on foot, and they ain't no trains comin through here until after midnight. We goin to get the niggers, I tell ya that right now. I'm gonna go down that pond now, look around, see if that knife layin around down there. I'll have em fore sundown, Red. I'll have them niggers, ya count on it."

3

It did not take much to make Shorty happy. James Harris "Shorty" Anderson always had a smile on his face. Folks say he went to bed with it, slept with it, and woke up with it too. Everybody liked Shorty. He wasn't much bigger than one of them midget people in that travelin show that came to Banes a couple years back. Shorty's close to sixty now, but still got the quick hoppin walk, looks like he's bouncing stead of walking, but he always smiling. Down there at LeRoy's place, Shorty be hoppin to that music, smiling, sweating, and shining. You could not help but look at him.

Shorty lived down in the Patch, lived up behind Reverend Sims' place, you had to go through Reverend Sims' dirt yard to get to that little shack Shorty stayed in. Town folks had taken a likin to Shorty a long time ago, got used to his "Good mawnins" on rainy days. Shorty got his own little business like, works up there in town, doin all kinds of things, sweepin here, moppin there, runnin packages over that way, everybody knew where to find Shorty, here, there, or just call him and he come runnin and smilin.

Saturdays were good for Shorty, town folks be payin what they owed him, folks be in a good mood, liquor be startin to flow, and nighttime be comin. He'd usually stay up town till the shoppin stores close, that would be about five o'clock, then he come down Front Street, turn there at the courthouse, and scoot down Dillion Street past them Saturday-night places, cross them tracks, get on the Patch Road, and bounce across the Catfish bridge. Patch ain't far from there.

It's not five o'clock yet, Shorty doesn't know what time it is. Sun still high and hot, but Shorty is just a bouncin down Dillion Street with that smile on his face. When he gets across the tracks, he looks back over his shoulder, then almost stumbles but keeps the smile on his face and that talk he's carryin in his mind. He hurries his hop. He got some talk Patch folks ain't heard yet, some talk that might have to be whispered first.

Reverend Sims spent his Saturday morning readin that Bible of his, you could always find him up on his sittin porch with that Bible in his hands. He had two Bibles, the one he readin and won't let nobody touch and that one he holds and gets to slammin down at Sunday church. That one he don't let folks touch or read, he say came through slavin time, he say his daddy carried up from slavin time, said his daddy learned the Word from it. Reverend Sims had a good livin that showed on him. Kept some chickens and pigs up in the sheds out behind his place, had more of everything than most Patch folks had of anything, except LeRoy.

Reverend Sims had some years too, that hair he had left was cotton-white, but when he got to preachin and jumpin up and down at the old Patch church with that sparkling sweat just a rolling down that deep-black face of his, you'd think he was just born.

Things and time had a certain way of moving in the Patch. Folks had their predictable ways, could tell who was who by the way they might bang a cookin pan or yank an outhouse door closed, even how they might carry a night-light, which way it swung might let you know who was swinging it.

Reverend Sims put his Bible down when he saw Shorty bouncing up the road, then stood and took his Bible in the house, put it away, and came back out onto the sittin porch and waited for Shorty.

"Reverend, Reverend, hey, Reverend." Shorty started shouting as soon as he seen Reverend Sims, then cut off the Patch Road and up through the side weeds and run up into the Reverend's dirt yard.

Shorty is at the bottom of Reverend Sims' sittin-porch steps looking up at the Reverend with that smile on his face. "Reverend, Ah's hearin somethin, hearin one of them little white girlchilds got stabbed, hear it's one of them childs of Mister Red's, that limp-walkin man that be livin out there past the waterlands. They come for Doc Grey, Sheriff Tom was way out past the hard road, soon as he gits back he goes flyin out there. They's still lookin for Mister Red, they's got to tells him. Ah was sweepin up in Mister Hanner's cuttin shop, that's wheres Ah hears it. That's where that talk was at. They start sayin some colored folks done did it, colored folks done cut that child. They thinkin it might be some of them freight-train-ridin coloreds might've drift back up in there from them tracks goes by out theres."

Shorty stopped talking, kept smiling and looking up at the Reverend. Reverend Sims stopped looking down at Shorty and looked out the Patch Road, then let his eyes wander a bit. Then he looks back down at Shorty, shakes his head some like he does in the Patch church, and says, "Lord have mercy, is she dead?"

"Folks ain't knowin, sorta waitin on Doc Grey to gits back. Doc Grey, he still be out there, and Sheriff Tom still be out there too," Shorty says, rocking back and forth like he does when he ain't walking and trying to stand still.

The Reverend takes one of them deep sighs, then blows that air out of his mouth so hard his lips start shaking. He looks down at Shorty and starts saying like he's praying, "Thunder in the sky, gonna bring lightnin in the night. What's wrong wit folks these days? Hurtin some child like that, God have Mercy." The Reverend gets his sweat-wipin handkerchief out and starts patting and dabbing at his forehead.

Shorty gets a chance to ask what he's been tryin to figure out. "Reverend, ya thinkin somebody down here done gone up theres and done that hurtin to that child?"

Reverend Sims just keeps wiping his forehead while he thinking like Shorty wants him to, then the Reverend shakes his head and says sharply, "Ah don't wants to hear that kind of talk around here. Folks around here gots they ways, but cuttin up on children ain't one of em, that ain't colored folks' ways, naw sir, ain't colored folks' ways to be hurtin white childrens like that."

Shorty left, started making his talkin rounds. Reverend

Sims went back into the house, got his Bible, came back out, and started sittin and readin again, but kept looking up and down that Patch Road.

Shorty figured he run down to the end of the Patch Road to LeRoy's place, see if anybody be down there sittin. Besides, he already had his sippin money and was thinkin to get him an early taste. Getting to LeRoy's place was quick and easy, you couldn't see it from the Patch Road, it sat so far back in the weeds and trees, but that path running back in there was so worn and stepped down, it could shine in the night. LeRoy's place was one big shack with an extra part he built on so he could set up a counter and keep him some whiskey behind. That's where Shorty found LeRoy sittin and already sippin and talkin with Lucy Mae and Big Jake.

LeRoy knew everybody, knew their names and how to call em, how to make em feel good about things. LeRoy was bigger than Big Jake, had that dark shiny skin but not a hair on his head. LeRoy could listen to some talk, good talk, bad talk, LeRoy could listen, but he could take you down too, tell you and the other folks standing around all about yourself. Even them Saturday-night white boys that come down there, get some drink and anything else they could get, kept themselves in line around LeRoy.

"What ya doin down here, Shorty Man? What ya doin here already? Come on over here and get yourself a little somin for this heat." LeRoy starts turning around and reaching for a drink for Shorty, but keeps talkin. "Yeah, what ya got for me today, Shorty Man, or ya just gettin ready to start your good time early? Getcha a little head start?" LeRoy's still pouring.

"Ah heard me somethin, hears it first," Shorty starts. "Ah was a sweepin up at Mister Hanner's cuttin shop and Ahs hears it up theres. Somebody done puts a knife in one of them little white childs, puts a knife in her out there past the waterland. Sheriff and Doc Grey be outs there now. They say it might be one of em driftin niggers comin off the tracks that do that, they . . ."

LeRoy spins around, looks down at Shorty's smilin face, puts the glass of whiskey down on the counter, and just keeps lookin at Shorty. Then LeRoy blurts out, "What ya talkin about? Where ya hear all this? Ya makin this shit up? What's wrong with ya, man? Come in here talkin all this shit wit that silly-ass grin stuck on your face, where ya hear this at? Ya best not be comin in here tellin no story, making shit up like ya's out ya mind."

Shorty starts rockin back and forth, grabs his drink, and gets him a fast sip and starts talkin up again. "Um tellin ya what Ah hears, Mister Macky tellin Mister Hanner, he tellin he was a talkin to Doc Grey whens they come to git him. Says they's told Doc Grey to grab his bag and come on. Mister Red's little girl been cut, and they says colored done dids it, that's what Ah hears. Soon as Sheriff Tom gits back, he turns that sheriff car arounds and goes flyin out there. They still out there, they's out there now."

Shorty shuts his words off, but keeps his mouth open and gulps his drink down.

LeRoy gets hisself another drink, Big Jake and Lucy Mae start giving Shorty what he wants, questions, until LeRoy burst in their talk and wants to know, "What time this here happen? They say how bad she cut?"

Talk went on, LeRoy left, and when he got back, the talk was still there. Shorty and them thought he just went out to the outhouse and didn't even notice when he pulled that big pistol of his out of his pants and slid it under the counter, right next to his head-knockin stick.

Lucy Mae had some talk now, she left Shorty, Big Jake, and LeRoy back there talkin. Lucy Mae was a big woman, had big ways. When she talked it was loud, when she walked she let the weight in her hips just sway. She had a big taste for that whiskey, had that taste for a while, could not and would not wait for Saturday night, had to have some every day. Patch folks knew her ways, knew she was takin Shorty's money off him, knew her and LeRoy been doin somethin. Patch folks sorta knew, that boy of hers, Gumpy, was sorta LeRoy's too. Lucy Mae still lived down there on the Patch Road with her mama, Esther Green. Her daddy, Wally Green, fell over dead in them pickin fields out at Hatcher's when she was just a baby, that was twenty-five years ago.

Cinder was sitting and reading one of them magazines she has. Every time she gets a little quiet time, she gets one of her magazines out and reads about people in faraway places. She likes those Hollywood movie people, and the big pictures of them in that *Life* magazine she's looking at.

Katey comes running up through the dirt yards, ain't saying nothin, just running until she gets close to the sittin porch and sees Cinder, then she starts yelling up to Cinder, "Child, we's got troubles, ya hear me? We's got trouble."

Cinder kept reading until Katey was on the porch standing above her with all that yellin, then Cinder closes the book and stares off to where the far land and the sky meet. Katey's a talkin, "Ah feels trouble comin, one of them damn-fool driftin coloreds put a knife in a white child overs there past the waterlands. Sheriff and everybody outs there. Everybody in towns knowin about it. They sent for Doc Grey and he out there now tendin to that poor child. Lord, what fool goes and does somethin like this? Have mercy, Jesus. Lord, thats poor child."

Cinder ask quietly, "Is the child dead?"

"They ain't says yet if she dead. They say she was just a little girl, just a child. Trouble comin, Ah's knows it."

Cinder gets up and goes into the house. It's her Saturday time, she doesn't need this botherin, and the way she walks, she lets Katey know it.

Gumpy had run down through them thick bushes by the pond, then ran as fast as he could when he reached the tracks and kept running, only slowing some to cross the train trestle. Then and only then did he stop and look back. Then he ran again, ran out in the openness of the tracks, ran out of the sunlight into the shade of the thick bushes, deep into the bushes, where shadows and silence lurk together. He had crawled and slithered over the long, dead log and hid behind its solitude, only peeping out at any sound.

It was silent. Everything in Gumpy's world was silent except time. Time rumbles in his mind, that same time when the hands reached and grabbed at him, when the yells and screams bit at his ears, when Billy got jumped. That same time had stayed in his mind, making his heart pound to a raging cadence.

"Hey, Gumpy, hey, Gumpy, hey, Gumpy." Gumpy jumps, then raises his head slowly and peers through the thick green of bushes. Billy is calling his name.

"Gumpy, Gumpy, hey, Gumpy."

He comes to his knees and peers down to the tracks, sees Billy walking along the rails shouting his name.

"Billy, Billy, up here. Ah's up here. Where's they at? They

comin after ya, they's chasin ya, Billy?" Gumpy whispers to
Billy.

Billy skips off the tracks and comes squeezing into the
bushes shouting, "Gumpy, Gumpy, where's ya at? Ah can'ts
see ya, where's ya at, huh?"

"Over here," Gumpy whispers.

"What's ya doin in here, huh?"

"Ah ain't wants them gittin me."

"They ain't comin."

"Theys git ya? Theys jump ya?"

"Theys gits me down, but Ah's git up."

"Theys come git ya again?"

"Theys can'ts git me, Gumpy, they's girls."

"Ya gots blood on ya face, they's got ya."

"Ah hit em back, Ah hit em good. Ah got em back,
Gumpy."

"They's got ya good, Billy, they's got ya good in the face."

"Ah got them Gumpy, theys can'ts keep me down."

"They were bigger, they could beat ya."

"Naw, they ain't, Ah gits up and gits them."

"Billy, theys beat ya, ya just ain't sayin so."

"Ah got em, Gumpy. She come gits me again, Ah
stuck her."

"Ya ain't stuck her, she bigger."

"Did so. Ah stuck her. Ah stuck her in her titty."

"She bleed? Ya ain't stuck her."

"She hollered, then she fell down. Ah seen her."

"Ya ain't did that, ya ain't stuck her none."

"Yeah, Ah did, look. See? Look at my knife."

Billy pulls the knife from his pocket and pulls its blade
out, then holds it up for Gumpy to look at.

"See, see? It still got blood stickin on it. See?"

"Ya stick her? Ya stick her deep, huh, Billy? She fall?"

"She come, tries and gits me again. Ah stuck her fast."

"Where ya stick her at? She fall down?"

"Ah tells ya, Ah stuck her titty and gits her arm too."

"She fall down? She gits back up? She still bein alive?"

"Ah tells ya she falls down. Ah ain't tellin ya no more."

"Ya kills her?"

"Ah tells her Ah kills her, she come botherin me again."

"She killed, they's goin ta chase us, Billy. Theys try and gits us."

"Ya scared, Gumpy, ya scared. They can'ts find us."

"Ah bet they's comin ta git us. They comin ta git us."

"Theys ain't chasin nobody. Theys ain't comin, Ah watched. Ah ain't seen em. Ya scared."

"Theys go and tells theys mama on us. Ah bets theys did."

"Gumpy, theys can'ts find us, they ain't knowin where we's live."

"They can come ta the Patch, look for us there, tell our mamas."

"We can hide. Theys can'ts find us, we can hide good."

"Where's we goin ta hide?"

"We can hides down by the Catfish, hides by that tree."

"What tree ya talkin about?"

"That tree, that big tree be fallin down, where them big cats be."

"Theys find us there, theys come see us there."

"Theys can'ts see us there, Gumpy, can't nobody see us there."

"Yeah, they can."

"Ya scared. Theys can't git us, we can git on a train, gits away."

"Theys go too fast. Ah ain't jumpin no train."

"Uh huh. We can jump on one of them old freights. Theys go slow."

Gumpy is silent, he looks away from Billy and lets his eyes peek down through the bushes and settle on the rusty-colored tracks. He stays quiet, but his eyes twitch and look up the tracks as far as he can see from his hiding place.

"We's can gits on one of em old freights, go ta Chicago, go ta Memphis, we can go everywhere, just ya and me. They's got picture shows all over, real big buildins, ya can look up and can'ts see where they end. Ah see em in my mama's lookin books," Billy shouts, excitedly, then nudges at Gumpy's back for him to turn around. But Gumpy won't look at Billy.

"Ah wants ta go home," Gumpy whimpers.

Patch dogs were scrawny-lookin dogs, most of them didn't have enough skin to cover their ribs good. Not all of them had names, some of them didn't belong to nobody, but they hang around just the same. Seem to know when to come around, sit till somebody throws them chicken bones out, or that chicken head. They seemed to know when somebody was about to kick at them, get tired of having them and their fleas hangin around, throw something at them, try and hit them, chase them away. Patch dogs had their ways too. If there wasn't nothin to eat, they sleep their days away, find some shade up under somebody's sittin porch, or them ones that didn't belong to nobody would get up under them road bushes and just lay.

"And after him was Semma the son of Age of Arari. And the Philistines were gathered together in a troop: for there was a field full of lentils. And then the people fled. . . ." Reverend Sims flinched, lifted his eyes from the Second Book of Kings, 23:II, when he heard the barking of the Patch dogs.

He closed his slavin Bible when he saw the red dust spiraling above the low trees and bushes that lined the distant Patch Road. He knew, as the dogs knew, somethin that wasn't belongin around here was comin.

Patch dogs started runnin down to the road, barkin and howlin on their way. Them dogs already down at the roadside was out in the road, barkin and growlin. Patch children stopped their play and just stood watchin the road. Porch-sittin mamas got up on their feet, moved out to the edge of their porch, stood watchin the road. Reverend Sims' wife, Netty, came to the door, then out onto the porch.

Sheriff Tom's big black Ford with that red dust stuck all on it comes rolling down the road with them dogs already chasin it.

"What he doin down here?" the Reverend's wife utters.

"Get in the house, woman." The Reverend snaps his words, then stands and comes to the edge of the porch.

The black Ford has slowed, the dogs and some of the children run alongside of it. It stops, then slowly moves on again, until it disappears down at the end of the Patch Road, where the bushes rise again.

Reverend Sims does not move, his eyes stay on the green thick bushes where they last saw the dusty car. Patch mamas started callin them children, each child seem to have its own sound callin for it. The dogs are returning to their places in the shade, but the Reverend is still. He knows the Patch Road doesn't go that far and there's only one way out of the Patch by car, and that's the same as the road in.

Shorty just a smilin and rockin, that whiskey just a rollin around in his head, got his mouth sayin everything. Big Jake ain't listenin, sittin over there sleep with his whiskey. LeRoy is just hafe listenin to Shorty. Shorty sayin the same thing anyway. Della Robinson is down LeRoy's too, she come down, heard Shorty down there with some money in his pocket, spendin it early. She has been tryin to get Shorty out of there, get him out back, and get some of that money before he spend it all on hisself. LeRoy knows what she's tryin to do, but he don't care, if the money don't come from Shorty's hand now, it will come from hers later.

"Hey, Shorty, baby, what's ya gonna do for Della, huh? Ya got somethin for me? Ya ain't hidin nothin, huh? Ya ain't hidin from me, are ya?" Della is cooing, and the more she does the more Shorty rocks and grins. "Come on ta me, Shorty baby. Why don't ya come on and goes wit me, Ah let you see some things ya like to look at. Ya like that, ya know ya likes to see some things Ah got for ya."

Shorty's eyes are dancing in his head. Della keeps cooing and giving Shorty some good long looks. She knows he so drunk now, she can take him out back in the bushes, let him put his face in her breast, show him a nipple, and have what he got left in his pocket. She got him now, got him sniffin right behind her and just about to get through the door when Sheriff Tom come bustin in.

Shorty starts smilin up in the sheriff's face and slobberin his words. "Afternoon, Sheriff Tom, fine afternoon, Sheriff."

Sheriff Tom pushes Shorty out his way and walks up to the counter.

LeRoy has stood, leaned over, and put his elbows down on the counter, looks at the sheriff, and says, "Ah got some bourbon here, ya want a little taste for this here heat?"

"Ya musta know I was comin."

"Figured ya might just stop down here."

"Ya knows why I'm here, then. I take it this little old boy here with that grin all over his face and that rotgut ya sold him, told ya about Red Pasko's little girl. Did he tells you about that? I'll take some bourbon."

Sheriff Tom made a little grunt as he stopped talkin, took his hand, and rubbed it across the back of his neck while LeRoy poured him a drink. Then he turned around and looked at Big Jake sittin and noddin, saw Della standing in the doorway with Shorty, trying to ease him out quietly, but Shorty ain't goin nowhere now, he wants to give Sheriff Tom some more talk. Sheriff turned back to LeRoy, picked his drink up, and, with one quick gulp, the bourbon was down, then he put the glass back down and said, "Gimme another one here."

LeRoy poured another drink for the sheriff and poured hisself one too.

The sheriff took a sip and wiped the back of his neck again and just stood quietly for a moment. LeRoy tilted his glass up, drank his bourbon down, poured hisself another drink, and filled the sheriff's glass back up.

"LeRoy, I got somethin ugly here, real ugly," Sheriff started talkin real slow, almost mumbling.

"Yeah, Ah hear, Sheriff. Shorty comes down and tells me somebody hurts a little girl," LeRoy says. Sheriff twist his thick neck around and looks at Shorty's smilin face.

"Yes sir, Sheriff Tom, good afternoon, Sheriff Tom." Shorty's words slur as he bounces his way over to the sheriff.

"Yes sir, Sheriff Tom, Ah hear it first, yes sir, Ah hear it down Mister Hanner's cuttin shop, yes sir, hear it there. Hear that little child gits hurt, and hear it some of them driftin coloreds that done it, yes sir, that's what Ah hears." Shorty finished talking but kept smiling up in the sheriff's face.

The sheriff turned back to the counter, took a sip from his glass, but could still feel Shorty's grin grinding against his back. Then, quicker than swatting a buzzin fly, the sheriff spund around and brought the back of his hand across Shorty's smiling face. Shorty's dwarflike body went hafeway across the room and landed on one of the tables, then he and the table crashed to the floor. Shorty just laid there, wasn't a smile on his face. Big Jake woke up and Della Robinson got out of there.

"Little girl ain't hurt, she dead," the sheriff mumbled, then turned back to LeRoy, saying, "I got somethin ugly here, real ugly."

"Umm, what can Ah do for ya, Sheriff?" LeRoy asked.

"I got me a little girl layin out there dead. She got a stab from a knife that let all her blood run out of her. She's dead. Wasn't nothin nobody could do for her once that knife was shoved up in her." The sheriff mumbled something that LeRoy couldn't hear, then was silent for a moment.

"I wanna know, which niggers did this?"

"Ah ain't heard nothin for ya, Sheriff, been here all day."

"That ain't what I asked ya, LeRoy."

"Ah ain't heard tell of it till Shorty bring it here."

"That ain't what I ask ya."

"Ain't nobody down here, cept Big Jake. He sleepin all day. Della come down here when Shorty git here. She ain't knowin nothin. Ah ain't heard of no driftin folks bein around. If Ah do, Ah come and gits ya myself."

"That ain't what I asked ya."

Silence.

Sheriff Tom leans from the counter, looks over to Big Jake, but doesn't say anything, then slowly walks towards the door, then pauses in the doorway, wipes the back of his neck, and turns around and looks at LeRoy.

"I reckon it's about four-thirty, five o'clock abouts. I want them two boys fore that sun goes down. I don't get em, I'm not even gonna be askin why. Ya hear me? Ya want ta fuck again, ya think about it," Sheriff Tom mumbled, but LeRoy heard him.

Reverend Sims' eyes went from the road to them bushes and high grass when the corner of his eye catches a glimpse of some quick jerky movement. He sees Della Robinson runnin with her hands flappin like bird wings, and watches her until she reaches the first shack at the road's end and disappears behind it. He waited. He could hear her voice shouting at the porch-sitters out back of the shack, but could not make out her words. When he could see her again, he stepped down his two steps and walked out into his dirt yard some, so she'd be sure to see him. He knew she would come to him. All sheeps come to the shepherd when wolves come, he thinks.

Della Robinson scoots up between the shacks and sees Reverend Sims standing with his hands folded, his ways call her to him.

"Reverend, Reverend, that sheriff, he just, he, he . . ."

"What happen, child, what ya tryin ta tell?"

"That Sheriff Tom be's down LeRoy's. Shorty ain't botherin him. Shorty wasn't doin nothin. Sheriff Tom takes his hand and just knock Shorty clears ways across them tables LeRoy got down there, takes his hand and just knocks poor Shorty for nothin. Hit him just likes ya knock a mule. Shorty just a layin down there, be layin down there on the floor, got blood comin all out his mouth. Then that old sheriff just turn on back arounds."

"Lord have mercy."

"Ah got on out of there. He say that child dead. After he smacks Shorty, he say that child is dead. Ain't no tellin what that fool man be doin now. Ah gits out of there."

"Lord have mercy. He say that child done died?"

"Ah hear him say that. He smack Shorty and that what he say."

"Ya just go on home now, git in the house."

The Patch dogs started barking and running down to the road. Reverend Sims turned and went back up his steps and went into his house, then closed the door.

Sheriff Tom's car came back up the road, the dogs chased it until it stopped, then they barked around its doors until the sheriff pushed the door open and got out. The dogs sniffed a little and backed away, growling and whining. The children had vanished.

The sheriff came around the car, and stood there with his hands on his hips while he looked up at the rows of shacks, then started up one of the paths.

Jackson Bivens was a sturdy-built man, young man still in his twenties, lived down there next to the Patch Road with his wife and their three children. Saturdays were slow for him, he had done some chores and was just sitting and waiting on eatin time. His wife, Tammy, wasn't too far from havin the fourth mouth to feed and was trying to keep the children quiet. They both knew Sheriff Tom was in the Patch, and that young white child was dead.

Jackson Bivens jumped when he heard the heavy footsteps come up on his porch. He got up and went to the door quickly but was pushed back into his sittin room by Sheriff Tom as the sheriff busted into the house. Tammy grabbed for her children as they ran and clung to her side. The youngest started crying.

Sheriff Tom stood in the doorway, the back light of the sun made him a massive faceless shadow.

"How many children ya got here, boy, how many, damn it?" Sheriff Tom's shout shook the sittin room.

"These here my children. These my children here," Jackson Bivens stammered.

Silence, except for the crying children and heavy breathin.

The sheriff looks around the room, then mumbles, "Ya got two boys around here that killed a little girl. I want em, ya hear?"

Out there behind the Patch, and behind Stony Mound, which wasn't nothin but a couple more shacks where some self keepin coloreds lived, was what folks called the Bad Land. About the only thing the Bad Land was good for was raisin snakes and water rats. It was too muddy for planting and living. Hafe swamp, the other hafe wasn't much more than clumps of hard mud with a few trees growing amidst them tall cattails. Bad Land had some zigzaggin little trails cutting through it, most of them led back to Stony Mound. Then that land between Stony Mound and the back of the Patch wasn't much better than the Bad Land. It didn't have all that water, just that thick muddy dirt. Its paths zigzagged around all through it, had to know just where you were, to get where you were going.

Billy and Gumpy knew the paths, and Gumpy knew which one would take him home, and that's the one he was on. They had cut through the bushes by the tracks, come through them thin trees over there and then crossed the Catfish Creek and zigged and zagged through the Bad Land, come around them Stony Mound fields and into them muddy fields behind the Patch.

Gumpy's leaning forward in his walk, has his head down, but he's not thinking of no snakes. Billy's lagging behind, stops sometimes to see if Gumpy is going to stop, then runs a little bit to catch up when Gumpy keeps going. Billy looks ahead, past Gumpy, and knows home ain't that far. He can see them brown back shacks of the Patch.

"Hey, Gumpy," Billy shouts.

Silence.

"Gumpy, Gumpy," Billy calls again.

Silence.

"Hey, Gumpy, come on, wait up."

"Naw," Gumpy shouts back.

"Come on, Gumpy, let's waits fore we's goes home," Billy shouts.

Silence.

"Ah goin home, Billy. Ah ain't playin wit ya no more, ya git us in troubles. Leave me be," Gumpy shouts but does not look back.

"Ya just scared, Gumpy, ya just scared of everything. Ya just a big old crybaby, ya older than me, ya twelves already, but ya still be fraids of everythin. Ah ain't scared, Ah ain't afraids, Ah show ya Ah ain't afraids of nothin. Ya fraid, not me. Hey, Gumpy, come on, wait up," Billy shouts ahead as he lags behind.

Gumpy starts running as he sees the Patch shacks. His eyes widen and the tears begin to bubble up in the corners. He reaches the back dirt yards of the shacks and begins to wind down through the paths until he reaches his home, then he runs inside.

Billy sighs as he watches Gumpy disappear into the shack yards, then begins to quicken his steps. When he gets to his home, he does as he always does, jumps up on the side of the porch.

"Thank Jesus, thank ya, Jesus. Here he is, he's home," Katey shouts as she hears Billy on the porch.

Cinder turns from the cookin table. She had calmly started the Saturday meal after Katey came runnin in the house screamin about getting all the children in because the sheriff hit Shorty and was down in the Patch botherin folks.

"Get in here, child, get in here." Katey gets Billy by the arm and pulls him into the house, then ask, "Where's ya been? We been just a worryin about ya. Where's ya get all them scratches on ya face? Let me look at ya, come over here."

Cinder yells above Katey, "Billy Lee, come over here now. Let me see your face. What happened to your face? You and Gumpy get into a fight? He hurt you like this, did he?"

"No, Mama, he ain't hurt me, we ain't fights," Billy answers his mother as she gently holds his face up in her hands and looks at the scratches and bruises.

"What happen to you, then?"

"Nothin, Mama, nothin."

"Billy Lee, did you and Gumpy have a fight?"

"No, Mama, no, we ain't fight."

"What happen to you, Billy Lee? Who scratched you?"

"Nothin, Mama, Ah fall in the stickin bushes."

Silence.

"Billy Lee, you been in a fight. Now, tell me, who hurt you like this? Somebody scratched you real bad, who hurt my baby?" Cinder ask in a whisper as she leans closer to look at Billy's face and turns it from side to side.

"Mama, Ah just fall in them bushes, them ones down by the Catfish, them real sticky ones," Billy says again.

"You been in town, did you get in a fight in town? I told you not to go in town. Were you in that town?" Cinder ask quickly.

"No, Mama, Ah ain'ts go in the town, Ah ain't goes there."

"Where were you, then? Answer me, where were you, Billy Lee?"

"Lord, what's goin on outs there?" Katey shouts and runs to the door and peeks out, then jerks the door open and runs out onto the sittin porch. Cinder and Billy Lee follow. "Have mercy, Jesus, have mercy. What's that man doin? My God, that's Gumpy he got draggin, that's Gumpy he gots." Sheriff Tom is dragging Gumpy down to the Patch Road, and Lucy Mae is cryin and screamin behind them.

Cinder stares but does not blink. Quickly she grabs Billy's arm and jerks him into the house. Her whispers are hurried, "Billy Lee, look at me. What happened, what did you and Gumpy do? Answer me, now."

"Some girl, she beat me up, she chase me, gots me down. She beats me up, she bigger too, she won'ts lets me go. Ah stuck her. Ah stuck her for her to lets me go, then Ah runs." Billy's voice is quivering, tears burst from his eyes. "Mama, is the sheriff gits me, huh? Mama, don'ts let him gits me."

Cinder cringes and pulls Billy close to her, but quickly looks towards the door. Everything has its own sound now: Billy's tears, the pounding beneath her breast, the squeaks of the floorboards under her feet, the stillness of the hot sticky air, the fly on the window buzzing to get out, the fly on the screen door buzzing to get in. But it's the sound of Katey's screams that come crashing into her mind.

"Lord, Jesus, Jesus, he comin up here. He throws Gumpy in thats car and he's comin up here. Cinder, Cinder, he's comin up here," Katey screams.

Cinder firmly grips Billy's shoulders and pushes him out from her, then quickly leans down and looks into his eyes. She whispers, a piercing whisper that must get through his tears, must get into his mind, must get into his heart, must get to him as quickly as it leaves her.

"Billy Lee, listen to Mama, and do just as I say. Get out of that window behind Mama's bed, run across that field, and get in them bushes where the Catfish turns. You stay there. Don't you come out till you hear me call, just me, you hear Mama?"

"Mama, Sheriff gits me? He comes and gits me too?"

"No, you hide till night. Mama come, you hide till Mama come get you. Here, take this blanket, and take this to eat. Now go, run, baby." Cinder has given a blanket, food from the cookin table, but has not been able to hold him tight. She pushes Billy through the window and shouts behind him, "Run, Billy Lee, run."

She watches him start across the field, then she turns and rushes for the door as Katey comes running in.

"He's comin up here. He's comin for Billy, Ah's knows it, he's comin here. Lord help us. Cinder, he's goin ta git Billy. What we's goin ta do?" Katey's muffled shouts fill the room, but Cinder is silent. She moves through the room with the swiftness of a cat, her dark eyes become darker, like burning wood before it begins to glow.

"God have mercy, child, what ya doin? Don't goes out there. What ya doin, Cinder? Cinder, oh Jesus," Katey shouts as Cinder swishes past her.

Sheriff Tom comes rumbling through the dirt yard and stomps up the porch steps. The shack door opens slowly and Cinder steps out onto the porch.

"Get out my goddamn way, where's that nigger at?"

"What do you want here? What do you want?" Cinder's eyes glow red, she stares into the sheriff's eyes, and her words hiss through the heat. "What do you want?"

Sheriff Tom pushes her aside and storms into the house yelling, "Where's that little nigger at? Where's that boy at, ya got that Billy Lee in here? Billy Lee. Billy Lee. I know ya here."

Katey comes running out of the house and into the dirt yard. Patch folks peek out their doors and windows and flinch at every crashing sound and yell coming from Cinder's house.

The sheriff's face is twisted, his teeth are gritting, his eyes flash back and forth as he jerks his large head from side to side. Everything in the house has been turned over, sleeping beds turned upside down and their feather mattresses kicked across the room. *Life* magazines are strewed over the floor. Pictures of people in long evening gowns, black tuxedos, big smiles on their faces, lay scattered over the floor.

The sheriff comes stomping back out onto the porch, his lips are pulled back from his tobacco-stained teeth, he spits out his words. "Where's that boy at, where's he at? I want that nigger and I want his little knifin ass right now. You his mama? Answer me."

"Naw sir, Ah ain't his mama," Katey whimpers up from the yard.

The sheriff turns quickly and looks at the woman who stands glaring up at him.

"You his mama, that boy yours?"

Silence.

"Answer me when I'm talkin to you. You that boy's mama?"

Silence.

"Where's that boy at? Ya his mama? Ya better answer me."

Silence.

"You that boy's mama?" The sheriff lowers his voice and slowly walks over to Cinder.

She does not turn from his snarling face, she does not flinch from his flexing muscles. She can smell the liquor on his breath, smell the scent of his sweat, but she is silent and only stares up into his eyes.

"Where he at?" The sheriff's eyes come to Cinder's.

It is silent.

"Goddamn you, bitch," the sheriff mumbles. His hand comes smacking across Cinder's face, knocking it to the side, but she jerks it back and throws her eyes back into his. Again his hand comes smacking across her face with the grunt of "Ya snake-eyed bitch."

Cinder is flung from the porch, lands, and skids on her side in the dirt. She lays with her face nestled in the ground.

Katey screams, prays, pleads, "God, leave her be. Don't hurt that child, please, don't hurts her. Good Lord Jesus, please don't hurt that child no more."

Sheriff Tom comes to the edge of the porch, watches the older woman run to the side of the woman he just knocked off the porch. Then he comes down the steps and slowly walks to where Cinder lays, then stops and just stares. Cinder pushes herself up, pushes Katey away, and throws her eyes back into the sheriff's face. Her hair hangs over her cheeks, blood seeps from her lip and nose, the skin on her cheekbone is scraped raw, but she still stares.

Sheriff Tom steps back, glances at the ground, then throws his head back up and mumbles, "I'm goin get that boy, I tell you that."

He leaves.

Cinder's eyes follow him down through the Patch paths.

She is silent.

4

Fred Sneed spent most of the time he figured he had left just sittin. Most of the time, town folks could find him sitting out front of the Rosey Gray, that little diner down on Front Street across from Macky's store and Mister Warden's place. Fred was known for his sittin, and was pretty good with them checkers if he could find somebody to play him. This Saturday was about same as most for Fred, the hot sun felt good on his old bones. His sittin buddies, the rest of them Banes old men that could talk your ear off, were inside the Rosey Gray. Fred told them he be in, in just a bit, wanted to sit awhile. Fred liked watching things, watching and figuring who was goin where and who was doin what. Fred started scratchin the side of his head a little, spit some tobacco out, and watched Evan Dorman bring Mister Warden's covered delivery truck around and pull it right in front of the door, then get out and go inside. Fred started to get up and go in the Rosey Gray, but figured he'd wait a bit. Pretty soon he knew he'd figured things out. He stood, took his sweat-stained hat off, and held it at his heart as he watched Evan Dorman and Mister Warden carry the white coffin out of Warden's burial shop and slide it into the back of the truck. He kept standing until the truck pulled away and headed out of town. Now he could go into the Rosey Gray and tell them somebody died.

Doc Grey drove into town, pulled his car up in front of his office, when Mister Macky comes running up from his counter shop asking, "How she doing? She gonna be all right?"

"Couldn't do nothing for her. She was gone when I got there."

"My God, Henry, she's dead? She wasn't but a child."

"Looked like that knife got in there just far enough."

"My God, Henry."

"Folks out there ain't taking it too good, barely holdin up."

"I heard it was two niggers, off the tracks."

"It ain't looking that way now."

"What ya mean, Henry?"

"Sheriff thinks it some Patch boys."

"Can't have these kind of ways startin up, no sir."

"Sheriff out there at the Patch now, lookin for em."

Matt Woodson came into town and went right down to Dillion Street, pulled his truck up behind Jack's place and went in the back door. Judy Fremont came over to him. He leaned over to kiss her, but she lowered her head.

"What's wrong, don't ya want my kisses anymore?" Matt teased.

"Red Pasko's little girl Lori been killed."

"What?"

"He was in here when they come for him. Niggers did it."

Harvey Jakes sat behind his desk. His week was over and another paper was out, not a bad one either. He sat reading over it, looking for them misprinted words he may have missed; so far it was pretty clean. Harvey Jakes, the editor and publisher of the Banes County *Times*, started publishing back in 1926. The staff had gone home, this was his time to reflect on the entire week. Harvey was in his late thirties, well dressed, still lived around the corner with his mother. Harvey's secretary and typist, Helen Marks, was probably the prettiest girl in town, or, if not, she had the longest legs. When she came running back into the office, Harvey couldn't help but keep his eyes on her skirt flying up over her knees until she scooted around his desk and yelled, "There's been a murder, Mister Jakes. A little girl been killed, I just heard it. Mister Hanner was talkin about it, said some coloreds did it."

Gumpy could not hear the things around him, could not hear the screams and shouts, the barking dogs. His own screams and cries would not let distant sounds in through his wall of fear. He had never been in a car before, and when it started up and jerked forward his stomach surged.

"Shut up back there." The sheriff's shouts seemed to shake the car from side to side. Gumpy had slouched down in the corner of the back seat when the car lunged forward, then lunged again as it shifted into second gear. Gumpy's eyes popped open. He peered through his tears and the glaring sunlight coming through the dirty car windows. Blue sky was moving, green treetops went flying by, then the sky was going by again, then the air came blowing in like wind before the rain. The car jerked again and the windy air teased his tears, smeared them over his vision, making everything blurry gray. He closed his eyes. Now only the image of the big fat neck and bull-like head of Sheriff Tom stayed in his mind.

The sheriff slowed the car and eased it over the small wooden bridge that goes over the Catfish, slowed again as he crossed the tracks, then sped up Dillion Street and turned left on Front Street. As a habit, his eyes always scanned the sidewalks, looking here and there. Most of the time, town folks just went on about their business unless there was a Saturday-night fight brewin, then they stop and stare as they do now. When he pulled into his parking space in front of the jail, Cecil Hill, his part-time deputy, and Stewart Ross, Cliff Whitman, and Frank Ottum came rushing up to the car.

"You get em, that him?"

"Just got this one, got one more out there," Sheriff shouts back.

"There another one still out there?" Frank Ottum shouts.

Silence.

"Sheriff, ya sayin ya got one more out there?" Frank Ottum shouts again.

"We gonna get him in a bit, Frank," Sheriff mumbles.

"We can go out there with ya, Sheriff, get that nigger out of there. We can help. Can't have that nigger runnin loose," Frank Ottum shouts.

Silence.

"Sheriff," Frank Ottum shouts.

"I'm goin ta get him, Frank. I'm goin ta get him in a bit,"

Sheriff mumbles, then pushes the car door open and gets out the car. Frank Ottum, Stewart Ross, Cliff Whitman go to the back of the car and peer into the window. The sheriff pushes them aside, opens the back door of the car, reaches in, and snatches Gumpy out the back seat.

"Get your ass out of here," the sheriff yells, and yanks Gumpy from the car and starts dragging him by the arm towards the jail.

"How old's that nigger, Sheriff?" Frank Ottum shouts.

Except for Gumpy's gasping and sniffles, it is silent.

"How old is this nigger? That other nigger still loose. Ya got his name? This here boy tell ya?" Frank Ottum shouts.

Silence.

"Cecil, get that bottom cell ready," Sheriff says.

"Got it, Sheriff," Deputy Hill answers quickly.

"Sheriff, when ya goin back out there to get that other one?" Frank Ottum asks.

Sheriff Tom drags Gumpy towards the jail and doesn't look back until he hears Frank Ottum shout, "Sheriff, it ain't right leavin that other one out there wild, we got children and women at home too." Sheriff Tom just stares at Frank Ottum, then turns and yanks Gumpy through the jail's door.

All the tears Gumpy has fall from his eyes now, as he looks around at the big walls, the big chairs, the big wooden fence that runs across the room. The big hand around his arm jerks him through the gate in the wooden fence, then flings him down into a big brown chair.

"Sit down here and shut your goddamn mouth, ya hear? Shut that goddamn cryin up, ya hear me?" the sheriff yells, then goes around his desk and sits in his chair. Gumpy sits with his head hanging down and staring at the floor.

The sheriff takes a few deep breaths, then rubs the back of his neck and looks at Gumpy.

"How old're ya, boy?"

Gumpy is silent, then starts to whimper, but keeps his head down. The sheriff ask again, but this time he lowers his voice and speaks softly, "How old're you? Come on, now, you can tell Sheriff Tom."

Gumpy is silent, then mumbles something through his whimpers.

"I can't hear ya, now, you gotta talk up, now. Come on, now, tell Sheriff Tom how old ya be." The sheriff raises his voice a little.

"Ah twelve," Gumpy whispers.

"Ya sure ya ain't fourteen, maybe fifteen?"

"Naw sir, Ah twelve, Ah was twelve at springtime," Gumpy whispers.

"What they call ya, huh? What's ya name?"

"Gumpy."

"What's ya full name, your last name?"

"Gumpy, they just call me that."

"Ya got a last name, boy? What's ya mama's name, huh?"

"Lucy Mae."

"Lucy Mae. What's ya mama's last name, what they call her?"

"Lucy Mae Thomas, she say my name is Roy."

Deputy Hill shouts from the cellblock door, "Sheriff, I got that cell squared away, you want me to take his black ass down there now?"

Sheriff Tom looks up, then glances at the clock on the wall and yells back, "I tell ya what I want ya to do for me, how bout goin over the Rosey Gray and gettin me a big roast beef, get me a soda too, and, Cecil, make that two."

The sheriff looks back at Gumpy and asks, "Boy, you eat today?"

Gumpy is silent, but squirms in his chair.

The sheriff looks back up at Cecil, and yells, "Get two, and better get yourself one too, we got a long night comin up here. Anybody got a lot of questions over there, ya just tell em we got the one and be gittin the other one right shortly. That's all ya tell em, ya hear?"

"You got it, Sheriff," Cecil yells back and goes out, leaving the gate swinging behind him.

Gumpy begins to raise his head but does not look at the sheriff.

"They call you Gumpy, huh?"

"Yah sir."

"What that other boy's name, what's he called?"

"Ah ain't did nothin. They chase me and Ah runs." Gumpy's voice raises.

"Who chased ya? What they chasin ya for?"

"We be in the pond, lookin for redbacks, Billy Lee say redbacks be in there, we be in there, then they comes after us, Ah runs, she chase me, but Ah, Ah gits away and runs. Ah ain'ts did nothin. Billy Lee, he say they gits him down, but he gits up. Theys were goin ta beats me up too, but Ah run," Gumpy blurts out.

"Billy Lee, that's your friend's name?"

"He ain't my friend all the times, just sometimes."

"How old's Billy Lee, he twelve too?"

"He ain't twelve, he ain't twelve like me."

"How old he be?"

"He ten, he say he eleven, but he ten."

Sheriff Tom sighs, rubs the back of his neck, gets up from his chair, and goes to the window and stares out into the street, then turns back and looks at Gumpy and asks, "What they call Billy Lee, what's his last name be?"

"Billy Lee, Billy Lee Turner, he say it's that."

The sheriff was goin to sit back down, he'd walked away from the window and was about to set, when the outer door opened. He looked over quickly, knowing it was too soon for Cecil to be back with the sandwiches. Harvey Jakes walks in.

"Sheriff, Sheriff Tom, hear we got a murder," Harvey Jakes shouts across the room and hurries up to the wooden rail with his pencil and notepad in hand.

The sheriff squints his eyes and just stares for a moment.

Gumpy goes to turn around in his chair, but slides back down in it when he hears, "Turn around, ain't nobody tells ya to move." Then he crosses the floor with rumbling steps until he gets up to Harvey Jakes.

"What ya doin bustin in here like that? Don't ya see Ah got a prisoner in here interrogatin?" Sheriff shouts in Harvey Jakes' face.

"I want to know what this is about, Sheriff. Did that boy there kill the Pasko girl? Folks are saying there's another one too. Is this the one that did the killing?" Harvey Jakes glances over the sheriff's shoulder and then quickly asks, "How old's that boy?"

"I ain't got time for this newspaper shit, I got to get done talkin to this boy," Sheriff shouts.

"Well, what can you tell me now? Is that the one did it?" Harvey Jakes glances over the sheriff's shoulder again, then blurts out, "Sheriff, how many times was she stabbed? What's that boy's name there?"

"Look, I told ya I don't have time for this here right now."

"Folks are talkin up a storm. I got to know what's goin on now, who is that boy? Is he a Patch boy?"

"Get your ass out of here now. When it's time, I'll let ya know."

When Deputy Hill got back with the sandwiches, he was surprised to see the sheriff sitting at his desk alone, and asked quickly, "You stick him down there already?" Sheriff Tom kept his head down and kept scribbling something with that two-inch pencil he keeps in his shirt pocket. Cecil moved quietly up to the sheriff's desk and put the bag of sandwiches down, then asked again, "Sheriff, you take him down already?" The sheriff sighed and just shook his head yes, then mumbled without looking up, "Take that boy down a sandwich, just stick it through, don't say a word ta him."

When Cecil got back up from feeding the prisoner, the sheriff was still sitting and scribbling with that pencil of his. "What ya thinkin, Sheriff?" Deputy Hill ask, taking a bite out of his sandwich.

"Gotta get that other one. He did the killin."

"You thinkin he got far. We can get Evan's dogs."

"Won't need that ta flush him out. He ain't far."

"That's that Bad Land out there, nigger could be anywhere."

"He ain't, he ain't that far at all. His mama hidin him, he ain't far."

Deputy Hill was quiet for a while, didn't know what to say, didn't even look at the sheriff, just noticed he hadn't touched his sandwich, but he looked up quickly when he heard the sheriff clear his throat, then mumbled, "We got somethin ugly here, real ugly. Got us a little girl layin out there dead that shouldn't be. We'll get the nigger."

Deputy Hill is silent.

The sheriff sighs, and mumbles quietly, almost at a whisper, "That boy ain't far. We're goin ta wait a bit, let him come out his hole. Wait till it gets good and dark, he'll come out or his mama will go for him, one or the other. We'll wait."

"You think he'll stay put that long?" Deputy Hill asks quickly.

"Boy ain't but ten years old, Cecil."

Down on Dillion Street, at Jake's place, Matt Woodson sat in the back booth with Judy Fremont. They had been seeing one another for two or three years, Judy been waitressing there since she got out of school. She was a quiet girl and still shy, it took Matt Woodson six months just to get her eye. When Frank Ottum came in, Judy got up and went into the kitchen. Frank Ottum been drinkin all day and came in throwin his words all over the place. "Got a nigger runnin loose out there killin. Still got that knife on him, ain't no tellin what a nigger goin ta do when they get wild like that. They get a taste of blood, get that killin in them, they come at ya. Come at ya like a wild dog. He down around that Patch, someplace, but a nigger like that will move on ya anytime."

Matt Woodson thought about Judy and how on edge she was about Red Pasko's little girl being killed. He got up and walked up to Frank Ottum, who was a good fishin buddy of his father's.

"Frank, I heard the sheriff got that nigger," Matt said.

"He got one of em down there, but that ain't the one that did the killin. He even admits it, that other one's still out there."

"Well, what's he goin to do?"

"Ya know how he is, all closed-mouthed about his business, he ain't sayin. Ah told him we got women and children around here."

Harvey Jakes was back at his newspaper office, Helen Marks had stayed late at his request. He had considered putting out an extra paper and might need her. Harvey's sitting at his desk, Helen's leaning against the rail that separates his office from the other desk and art tables. Harvey sits pondering the feasibility of getting the paper out, being so short-staffed.

Helen moves closer to his desk and leans up against it. She knows he likes to look at her legs, but what he didn't know is that she did not mind it. He was a very handsome man and had family money, plus some of his own. If she was never going to get out of Banes, then she was going to stay the way she wanted. Harvey Jakes could keep her in Banes the way she wanted to stay, but he was thinking more about getting his newspaper out than about her legs. She decided that, since he needed her now, she'd see to it that he would want her later.

"It's going to be the biggest story in the state, now, Mister Jakes. I'll stay with you. I don't have any plans except listening to the radio. I'd like to stay and help." Helen Marks spoke softly so as not to disrupt Harvey's thoughts but just to add to them.

Marcus Warden was an expert, and looked at his craft as an art. He'd been burying Banes folks since nineteen fifteen. Back then he'd get that big team of horses he had, hook them up for them big funerals, but wasn't too many of those. The little funerals, he just got one horse on that wagon, put that empty coffin in the back, go out there, and do what he could do with the body so it would last in the heat through sittin time. Most folks just brought the coffin and did their own buryin. Some folks didn't do that, just made a box themselves, and the heat would let them know when buryin time was. Nevertheless, Marcus Warden would come if he was sent for, and he'd spend the time that was needed to prepare the deceased for their last days aboveground and the first day of their eternal peace.

Mississippi suns set slow. The last sun that Lori Pasko saw, smiled under, fussed under, dreamed and giggled under, was setting as she cooled on her mother's bed. The porch was quiet. David, Kevin, and the younger boys sat leaning against the porch rail. Jenny's mother had come and set with Jenny in her arms. Ginger and Red Pasko sat on the porch steps; neither one had said a word in hours. Doc Grey had left, saying he'd send back Marcus Warden.

The Pasko dogs started barking, out of habit, then stopped but kept their eyes on the car coming up the dirt road. Ginger sighed and reached for her husband's hand as the car pulled up to the house and stopped. Elson Pittman got out.

Elson Pittman was a tall man, stood about six foot five, lean and slender and carrying his sixty years well. He wore black all the time and had silver hair and dark-blue eyes. He would always have his Bible, and kept its ways. He had a look about hisself, a look that others swayed from but could not turn from. He comes to the Paskos now and stands before them as they sit with their grief.

"Brother Red. Sister Ginger. Children," Elson Pittman speaks.

"Brother Elson, thank you for comin," Red Pasko murmurs.

"I've been sent by the Lord, it is His will."

Red Pasko sighs and Ginger grabs his hand, they both rise and step towards Elson Pittman, then their heads seem to bow and they stand silent.

"The eyes of the Lord are upon this house. He is here with

ya, He knows the sorrow ya bear here today. He knows. He sees. He hears. Where does the child lie?" Elson Pittman asks, then follows Red and Ginger Pasko into the house and back bedroom where Lori lays covered. They stand at the door as the tall man goes into the room, stands silently at the side of the bed. Ginger Pasko clutches her husband's hand and continues to squeeze it as Elson Pittman bends over and gently pulls the cover from Lori's face. Only her hair has the color of life.

The shades had been drawn in the room where Lori lies, the late-afternoon sunlight coming through the window is weakened and lets the darkness cuddle up in the corners. Elson Pittman stands erect, then tilts his head upwards. Ginger and Red Pasko remain standing in the doorway, but bow their heads as Elson Pittman begins:

"Lord, here lays this child, this beloved child. Let us not grieve for her taking, but rejoice that she is in Your kingdom now.

"Let us rejoice that she is in her Father's house. Let us cast our grief and grasp our exultation that the Lord Almighty God has called, that His hand has come so close, that His fingers have chosen so carefully.

"And she saw two angels in white, sitting one at the head and one at the feet where the body of Jesus had been laid.

"Let us not forget the stones that have been cast away. Let us not forget all powers are in Thy hands. All wills are Thy desires. She is with You now, Lord. Let us pray."

Red and Ginger Pasko returned to the porch and sat quietly again. Ginger's thoughts became stilled, she just stared. The sun was giving up on the day, the far skies glowed red. Mary Curran, Ginger's sister-in-law, was here now. She'd embraced Ginger, then went to the younger children, gathered them, and now sits with them. Herman Pasko, Red's brother, has come with his wife, Susan, they're doing the things that must be done.

Roy, Lori's youngest brother, who will turn five soon, is looking for the angels to come to take Lori for a ride, ride her up into the sky like Aunt Mary has told him. He sits looking to the red glowing corner of the sky. In his mind he can see the pretty white wings of angels fluttering amidst the clouds, but only Marcus Warden comes.

5

Saturday night is a good sittin night in the Patch. Folks have their own style of sittin. Old folks set back, might be rockin in a swayin chair, might have some kind of fan they done made, keep it on their sittin chair till they get to sittin. Them folks that ain't that old, maybe too old to go down LeRoy's place and be shakin all over, twistin their butts and jumping to that music, but ain't too old to get that sittin-porch hollerin done, keep it goin for a long time. These folks have their way of sittin too, might be on the steps, might be even standin too, but them shouts be goin back and forth, talkin about the same thing, just tellin it different ways. Young Patch folks too young to be down LeRoy's, and them that ain't snuck down there and hid in the bushes to watch all that goin on, they

79

runnin back and forth up and down them Patch paths, tryin to catch each other or a firefly.

But this night is quiet. Field birds have settled, Patch dogs lay quietly, night lanterns are dim if lit at all. Saturday, August 21, is fading.

The night silence in the Patch has its own sound, it is like a hum that you can't tell where it comes from, don't know what it is. Not listening for it, you don't hear it. You don't think about it until it is shattered by a cry, a quick bark of a dog, a bullfrog's belch. Then you wait for it to come back, shiver until it does, shake, thinking it might go away again.

Reverend Sims sits quietly on his porch. He sits in the dark, has told his wife not to light the lantern. He thinks about tomorrow and the sermon he will give, what he will have to say, then he worries about Gumpy and Billy Lee. He thinks of the faceless white child that is dead, he curses Billy Lee and Gumpy. He thinks of Cinder and shakes his head, then thinks of Sheriff Tom and looks out into the night and just stares.

Lucy Mae had screamed all day, cried and threw herself to the ground, had to be picked up and carried back in the house. Other women had come to her, tried to tell her Gumpy would be all right, Sheriff Tom would bring him right back, Gumpy didn't know what he was talkin about, children make things up. But Lucy Mae still screamed. Reverend Sims had come to her and prayed above her cries, let his voice be the word of his God. Other Patch folks went on back on their porches, whispered back and forth, said they weren't surprised that boy got in trouble, said if Lucy Mae paid him some mind stead of runnin down LeRoy's all the time it wouldn't have happened, said she ain't cared about Gumpy none since the day he was born and now she doin all that carryin on, didn't make no sense. Lucy Mae sits with her mother, she'd slumped down in her sittin chair still whimpering.

Jackson Bivens sits on his porch, his wife, Tammy, stands in the doorway holding her youngest child; the others she has forced to bed and silence. Tammy is not an old woman, just turned twenty-three, and has taken to Patch ways, taken well to her husband's ways, but now she quarrels with him, wants him to take them buckshot shells out that shotgun and put that shotgun up where it belongs. He keeps it under his sittin chair.

Della Robinson has told everybody what she saw Sheriff do to Shorty, how Shorty went to flyin through the room, how the sheriff said that little girl was dead. She was still talkin about it to Wesley Hall, but she was whispering now. Wesley Hall was the twenty-year-old field-pickin boy that lived next door to Della and was sitting with her in that back sleepin room of hers. She'd told him she wasn't goin down LeRoy's, wasn't goin out of her house no more this day, she wasn't wantin nothin to do with all this shit, these folks done turned pure damn crazy.

"Aw, come on, now, Della, ain't nothin gonna happen," Wesley Hall whispers with a smile on his face.

"Ya crazy? Ah ain't goin outta here, what's wrong wit ya?"

"Aw, come on, Ah can gits somethin for us."

"What can ya get? Ya ain't got no money."

"Yeah, Ah do too. What ya talkin bout? Ah keeps me some."

"Let me see what ya got, how much ya got, huh?"

"Ah got a nuff, got me nuff for ta sip all night if Ah wants ta. Now, come on, now, let's go down. We ain't gotta stay, just git us somethin and take it ta where it's quiet, where ain't nobody botherin us at."

"Ah ain't goin down LeRoy's. Ah done told ya that, Ah ain't goin."

"Aw, come, now, ya knows ya have a nice time."

"Ya better get out of here wit that, Ah done told ya."

Wesley scoots up to her, rubs his hand on her leg, tries to get it up under her skirt, and watches her dimly lit face for a smile.

"Ya better get outta here wit that shit, ya ain't gettin none of this tonight. Ah don't know what the fuck wrong wit ya, trying to pull this shit wit me. Ya ain't got the sense ya had yesterday, nigger."

Wesley's hand moves further.

"Stop it, Ah said."

Wesley moves away smilin, the sweat glistens on his face as he decides to play his last hand, the one he knows will win.

"Um goin on down LeRoy's, gits me a whole bottle, ya want me ta bring some back for ya? We can just drinks it here."

"Yeah."

Shorty has that smile back on his face, had a big busted lip with dry blood still stuck on it, but he was still talkin down there with LeRoy and Big Jake. LeRoy figured wasn't nobody comin out tonight and has fixed hisself, Big Jake, and Shorty something to eat, then maybe they'd play a little cards and see if he could get that little bit of money Shorty had left. Big Jake was almost as big as LeRoy, but had that high-yellow skin and low-talkin ways. He'd been pickin since he was seven, that was fifty-one years ago, had a wife and six kids and eighteen grandchildren. Folks say hafe them children in the Patch belong to Big Jake one way or the other. Everybody knows Big Jake, knows him for them pickin songs he be singin and them mules he could talk into movin, and if he couldn't get them to move he just pick them up and throw them.

Big Jake could pick him some guitar too, pick that thing till them strings turn fire-red. Big Jake ain't payin no mind to Shorty and LeRoy's talk, and ain't thinkin about Sheriff Tom. He's feelin good, got him something to eat and some of that good bourbon LeRoy pulled out for the sheriff. Big Jake ain't mindin this quiet night one bit as he picks at that guitar of his, hits them strings a few times, leans back in his chair and sips some more, hits them strings again, and waits till that sound curls into music and its echoes into a beat. He takes one more sip, then pulls that guitar up in his lap, takes his tongue and wipes his lips with it, and he ain't thinkin of nothin but that "Chitlin-Wigglin Girl" he be singing about.

Got me a little chitlin-wigglin girl
Wiggle her butt like a piggy's tail,
Ah hah . . . ah hah . . . ah hah . . .

Got me a little chitlin-wigglin girl
Got eyes that sparkle jus like a pearl,
Ah hah . . . ah hah . . . ah hah . . .

When she call me by my name
This old man he ain't the same
Ah hah . . . ah hah . . . ah hah . . .

Woke up one mornin, she was gone,
Wiggled her butt on into town,
Ah hah . . . ah hah . . . ah hah . . .

Ain't been back since that day,
Folks say she be gone ta stay,
Ah hah ... ah hah ... ah hah ...

Chitlin, Chitlin, wigglin, wigglin girl,
Come back here and bring ya wigglin tail,
Ah hah ... ah hah ... ah hah ... ah hah ...

Shorty still talkin, but LeRoy looks away and starts tappin his foot to Big Jake's singing, then stops, flinches, and looks towards the door.

"What ya doin down here? Ah ain't thinkin Ah'd see nobody out here tonight. Ya come down ta git ya a taste anyhow?" LeRoy grinned and shouted over to Wesley Hall coming through the door. Wesley glanced over and gave Big Jake a smile, then gave Shorty a nod and shouted back to LeRoy, "Shit, Ah though ya might be closed and be sleepin out back wit that shotgun, though Ah have ta git ya up till Ah sees ya lights, thens Ah hear Jake and Ah knows ya up."

"Ah ain't closin nothin tills Ah feel like it, come on and gits ya somethin," LeRoy grinned and shouted back.

"Gots ta git me somethin, can'ts be sittin witout nothin."

"Yeah, Ah thought ain't nobody comin down tanight, and here ya comes," LeRoy said as he got behind his counter. He poured Wesley a glass of some of that good bourbon and said with a grin, "Here, ya gonna like this."

Wesley took a quick sip, and in a moment said with a laugh, "Yeah, folks be up there sittin in the dark like they's the night theyselves."

LeRoy laughed back, then wanted to know, "What's Lucy Mae doin?"

Wesley took another sip before saying, "Last Ah seen her,

she sittin up there wit her mama. Ain't nobody seen Cinder, she up there in the house, ain't comes out since the sheriff knocked her ass off the porch. Lucy Mae's boy say that Billy Lee was bein up theres. Ah thought the sheriff be draggin him too, but he come out of there wit nothin but some mean on his face. That sheriff gots ta be thinkin Billy Lee done runs off someplace."

LeRoy shook his head and said, "Shit, where he gonna run ta? Cinder got that boy somewhere, yeah, that's what Ah thinkin. That woman got that boy somewhere. It's a wonder she ain't stuck a blade in that sheriff. Ya member that night she down here? Ya know how she gets, take her a little sip, might dance, gets ta movin all slow and twistin her ass all around, lookin good. She do look good. Ah remember she out there, got her ass up, everybody watchin. Then that boy Aldon, ya know how he gits, he don't mean nothin, but he tip up behind her while she dancin and goes to grind her in the ass. Well, shit, Ah mean, that bitch turn around and just give that motherfucker a look Ah ain't never seen nobody give. Ah mean, that bitch look like kin ta the devil. Most bitches just laugh that shit off or grind on back, specially when they done put their ass out in the first place, but, shit, not that bitch. She stared that boy down. Ah thought she be gettin ready to pull somethin out and cut the shit outta that boy. Didn't have to, though. Ah guess he thought he done tried to fuck the devil up the ass. Got away from her real quick." LeRoy was givin a little laugh, then sighed and said, "Yeah, that boy of hers ain't but, what, ten, twelve at the most."

Wesley Hall laughed and told LeRoy somethin he already knew. "Shit, that ain't too young for them ta takes a nigger, theys takes a nigger any size."

LeRoy grinned and shook his head until the grin fell off his face, then said, "Ah tells ya, theys come down here, Ah got somethin for em."

Wesley talkin quick now. "Ah's got ta gits back, gots me somethin waitin. Ah need me a bottle ta takes wit me."

Shorty's bouncing over in the corner by Big Jake, shaking back and forth with that music, but Big Jake ain't paying him no mind, had them fingers dancin on them strings faster than them words twistin through his lips.

The Patch night has its colors too, deep colors that seem to drift into one another, dark blues seeping into purples, misty grays floating while stars' yellows sparkle. Them tall trees along the far road stand dark gray above the black thick bushes beneath them. The road is dark until the bouncing lights come like cat eyes out of the night.

Reverend Sims stands watching the lights coming, he had heard the dogs barking, but now can only see the lights. The palms of his hands come together, he steps back from his sittin chair, then goes into the house and closes the door.

Jackson Bivens whispers to his wife, Tammy, "Git in there, ya hear me? Git in there," then reaches for his shotgun and closes the door.

Lucy Mae's mother stands and comes to the edge of her sittin porch, but keeps her eyes on the lights. Lucy Mae only turns her head, then looks back down at the porch floorboards.

Della Robinson hears the dogs barking, looks out the side window, then runs to the front door and looks out, closes it, and runs and gets under the bed.

Wesley Hall stops as the lights come bearing down on him, shining into his eyes. He clenches the bottle in his hands and stands still, then runs up into the shacks and crawls under a sittin porch.

Big Jake still sings. Shorty still bounces to the music. LeRoy still sips that good bourbon. They do not see the lights.

Reverend Sims hears the yells and shouts now, Lucy Mae's mother sees the lights become trucks and cars, then white men with sticks and guns. Then there are more lights, flickering lights of lanterns and fire torches. She grabs Lucy Mae and runs into the house and calls her God.

The silence of the night has run far into the darkness. Patch dogs howl. Harsh snarling voices yell and shout.

"Get that son of a bitch. Up in there, get im."

"Where's that knifin nigger, where's that bastard?"

"Turn this whole goddamn place over, we'll get him."

"Get that light over here. Spread the lights out."

"Where he at? Ya better get his ass out here."

"Fuck it, just burn it, he come out."

"Get outside here. All ya all up in there, get out here."

"Just pull im out, burn it if they don't get out."

"Search each one, spread out. Get a light here."

"Goddamn niggers, fuckin killin bastards."

"Where's that boy, where's that boy at?"

"Break it down, break it down, damn it. Get that light over here."

"Come on out of there, get out here, nigger."

"Got one under here, look, there's one hidin there."

Wesley Hall squirmed backwards, trying to get further back in the dirt beneath the porch. His mind went further than his wiggling body, his mind raced out of the night, far past the darkest dark, and just ran until it could go no further, then it came back cringing when the lights shined in his eyes and the sticks poked and dug into his sides.

"Get out of there, nigger. Get yer ass out of there, ya hear? Ah got him, Ah got his ass."

Shouts came under the sittin porch, then hands came and yanked Wesley Hall out into the flare of lights. Sticks beat at his back, then fists and clubs beat at his head, shouts come from all around like the flashin lights.

"Where's that knifin nigger? Where he hidin at?"

"Ah don't know. Ah ain't sees him. Ah ain't."

"Ya lyin bastard. Cut yer balls off, boy, ya don't answer here right."

"Ah ain't knowin. Ah's down Leroy's. Ah ain't sees him."

"What's his name, huh? What's that boy's name?"

"Billy Lee, he Billy Lee. That's his name, Billy Lee."

Lucy Mae's mother runs to the door and tries to keep it shut, but goes flying into the wall as the door burst open, her eyes squint at the waving lights and snarling faces.

"What ya all want here? What ya want comin here?"

"Who ya gots hidin back there? Get her out here."

"Ya all leave us be. We ain't dids nothin to ya."

"Get out here, woman. Get that other one out here."

Lucy Mae has come to the fire and lights, she has run through the house, and comes to her mother's side, screaming, "Where's my baby? Where's my baby? Ya got my baby? Where's Gumpy?"

Lucy Mae's mother grabs at her and shouts, "Get back in there, get back, shut up, Lucy Mae, get back."

"That's that one the sheriff got. This is that nigger's house."

"Ya got Gumpy, Ah want my baby, ya bring him back."

"Shut up, Lucy Mae."

"Burn that son of a bitch down."

"No, misters, please no."

"Bring my baby back."

"BURN IT DOWN."

The glare from the lights and fires shine through Reverend Sims' windows now, loud heavy footsteps come pounding up the steps and shake his sittin porch. Reverend Sims whispers to his wife, "Ya stay in here. Ya stay back in here. Ah sees what theys want." He goes to the door with his slavin Bible clutched in his hands. Lights flash across his face, shouts and yells smash into his ears.

"Ya got that Billy Lee in there? Where's that nigger at?"

"He is not here. This ain't his house."

"That's that preacher nigger, yank his ass on out of there."

The cries of the night went far. LeRoy knew he'd been hearing the dogs barkin, then the faint sound of screams wisp past his ear. "Shut up, Shorty, shut up," LeRoy shouted, then looks at Big Jake and whispers, "Jake, Jake, listen. Ya hear that?"

Big Jake stilled, listened to the night, then jumps up and heads for the door. LeRoy shouts after him, "Jake, where ya goin?"

Big Jake shouts over his shoulder, "Ah gots children up there, got my babies up there. Where ya think Um goin?"

"Fool nigger, shit," LeRoy hisses, then rushes to the night lamp, turns it out, and stands at the window, cursing the distant flickering fires. Shorty starts yappin about what he knows is happening. LeRoy tells him to shut the fuck up and then wades through the dark until he reaches his counter, his hand jabs beneath it until he feels the handle of his pistol.

On the path from LeRoy's, Big Jake's walk is steady, he

leans his shoulders into his stride, but his eyes stare ahead to the fires jumping in the night.

"Don't do it, put it down, they'll kill us, please," Tammy Bivens pleads with her husband, but he only whispers harshly, "God damn it, stay back there. Keep quiet." Now he stills hisself, but his eyes twitch with every approaching yell and shout. His fingers ease from the shotgun's trigger, his thumb gently pulls the hammer back until it locks itself, then he places his finger back on the trigger and waits for the door to come crashing open.

Della Robinson lays under her bed with her hands over her ears, she does not want to hear the shouts and screams coming from the night, but then the house shakes as the heavy footsteps thump up onto her sittin porch. Her door is bashed open, her bed is pulled and flung away, but her hands stay on her ears.

"Get her out, drag her. Get ya ass movin. Get up."

Della Robinson screams as she is being dragged across the floor, then she looks up into the faces of the men above her and pleads, "Leave me be. Please leaves me be, Ah ain't done nothin, Ah ain't bothered nobodies. Lets me be, please."

Big Jake comes into the light of the fires and lanterns, they swing his way, shine upon him, then gather around him.

"Get that big son of a bitch. Get him."

"Ah got childrens up there. Get aways from me."

"Get him. Get him. Get behind him."

"Get aways from me. Ya's hurt my childrens, Ah breaks yer necks."

Katey had screamed. Cinder had come to the window and looked, seen the car lights, then the fire torches burning. Now she stands in the dark shadows of her porch. Her eyes are keen, she follows the moves of the lights, listens to the shouting below, and shuts out Katey's cries and prayers from her mind. It is time now. She moves silently and swiftly off the porch and into the dark. She tiptoes until she's around side of the house, then she pulls her skirt above her knees and runs silently into the misty blacks and dark grays of the fields.

Sheriff Tom turns his big Ford off Front Street and onto Dillion. Deputy Cecil Hill sits in the passenger seat with his arm resting on the open window, but his eyes scan the sidewalks until the car passes Jack's place, then he turns around and looks back at Jack's place. "Damn, Sheriff, it sure looks empty for a Saturday," he says.

Sheriff Tom does not look back, does not say anything, just grunts and speeds the car up some.

"Ain't nobody seem to be out tonight, Sheriff," Cecil says again.

Sheriff Tom remains silent, but takes a deep sigh.

Deputy Hill will be twenty-six in a month, but still lives right outside of town with his mother. His father died a couple years ago, got that cancer and just shrunk down to nothin, that's when Cecil started helping out the sheriff in the evenings and Saturday nights. Cecil was a big man, built strong and solid, been working down the sawmill since he got out of high school, but his Saturday nights was what he looked forward to, no tellin what Saturday night might bring. He got used to Sheriff Tom's ways real fast, knew he could talk real slow, then knock the hell out of somebody while he was still talkin. Them Saturday-night crowds Jack's place got could get real unruly, didn't want to go home for nothin, get so drunk they forget who the sheriff is. Cecil knew the sheriff's ways, knew just to stand back and watch him go into one of them thick crowds and get right up in a loudmouth's face. That's when Cecil knew to just keep an eye on the crowd, make sure none of them boys tried to jump the sheriff from behind. Wasn't too many Saturday nights that someone didn't end up bein dragged out of somewhere, specially them boys come over from Greene County. The sheriff didn't talk too much, Cecil knew that, got used to not asking a lot of questions, but tonight was different and he had some questions, but couldn't ask them.

Sheriff Tom slowed the car and eased it over the railroad tracks, then sped up again. On the other side of the tracks the road narrowed and the bushes alongside of it were thick and grew up close to the road. The road took a few curves until it got to the Catfish bridge, then narrowed even more.

Deputy Hill dipped his head so he could look out the car's front window as it approached the bridge.

"Sheriff, Sheriff, look, somethin's burnin down there," Deputy Hill shouts.

Sheriff Tom drove on in silence.

"Sheriff, what's goin on down there? Look at that, that's in the Patch."

Deputy Hill quickly looked at the sheriff, looked for some reaction, listen for him to say somethin, make a grunt, mumble, but the sheriff was silent as the car rolled across the narrow Catfish bridge.

"What ya thinkin, Sheriff? What ya think that is?"

"God damn it," Sheriff Tom mumbled, then stomped down on the gas pedal. The car lunged forward once, and then seemed to rear back and lunge again as the sheriff quickly shifted gears.

The black Ford speeds.

The dark Patch Road becomes bright by firelight.

"God damn these fuckin assholes, god damn them," the sheriff shouts and slams on his brakes. The big Ford comes to a quick halt and rocks on its shocks and springs, is still rocking when the sheriff jumps out yellin, "What the hell ya all doin out here? Git outta here now. Let that nigger go, ya hear me, Ah said let him go. All of ya all, git outta here. Git the hell out of here now. Git over here, Frank Ottum. God damn it, Ah said git over now. Ah told ya ta keep ya ass out my business. Ya and the rest of these boys goin ta answer ta me, and ya ain't goin ta have the answers Ah want. Now, git ya asses outta here. Ya fuckin up my investigation. Um the law and ya in my law. Now, git outta here."

Frank Ottum shouts, "Sheriff, we got children too, can't have no wild nigger loose. We got a right, Sheriff. We got a right ta protect ourselves."

"Come here, Frank," the sheriff shouts, then starts to move through the gathering crowd of torchbearers. The men watch the sheriff come closer, Deputy Hill follows at a distance. Now the sheriff is whispering to Frank Ottum, "Come here, Frank. Come here, ya hear me?" He is close to Frank Ottum, so close that only Frank Ottum can make out what he is mumbling.

"Frank," the sheriff is whispering, "let me tell ya somethin that's gonna happen, Ah promise ya, if ya ain't outta my law, outta my way, if ya ain't outta my sight, Um not gonna kill ya, Frank, don't worry bout that. Um just goin ta blow your goddamn balls off, and every time ya try ta fuck ya can remember how ya got in Sheriff Tom's law. Now, Ah got my hand on my pistol. Ah don't have ta draw it, Ah just have ta tilt it. So what ya goin ta do, Frank?"

Frank Ottum backs away from Sheriff Tom and shouts to the surrounding men, "Come, let's go. Sheriff says he can git the nigger, says he'll have him in a bit." Then he calls to the sheriff, "Sheriff, ya need us, ya just call us, ya hear?"

Sheriff Tom mumbles, "Ah be sure ta do that, Frank."

Lucy Mae's mother stood outside her dirt yard holding Lucy Mae. She had called and called her God, now she is silent and only watches her home burn in the night.

Wesley Hall lays next to the road. He has crawled into the bushes and lays holding his side and gasping for air.

Reverend Sims had slithered around in the dark, found his Bible, and closed its pages, then limped to his sittin porch and set on the steps. His head is down, he does not look at the fire.

Della Robinson sat up in her dirt yard, staring down at the ground, and just kept trembling.

Jackson Bivens eased the shotgun's hammer back down and just set staring at his door with his hands still shaking. His wife, Tammy, has all the children gathered in her arms, and tries to cry quietly.

Big Jake plowed through the dark Patch paths and dirt yards, makin sure of his children. He has bruises on his arms and hands from beating off anyone that came too close to him.

LeRoy stands in the dark with his pistol in his hands. He can still see the distant fires. He does not know they are cooling.

Shorty stares through the window at the flames. The firelight dances in his eyes, he smiles.

Where the waters of the Catfish turn, it is quiet. Cinder whispers into the silence, "Billy, Billy, Billy Lee, it's Mama."

It is silent.

Cinder wades into the dark bushes.

"Billy, Billy, it's Mama. It's Mama, baby."

She stills herself and listens, but only hears night bugs

calling. She pushes the limbs and branches from her face before she whispers again.

"Billy, it's Mama, baby. It's Mama, Billy Lee, Billy Lee."

"Mama, Mama."

"Billy, Billy, where are you?"

"Mama."

She can see him now, she pushes through the bushes until
she can touch him, feel his face, bring him to her, and put
her arms around him.

Billy whispers into Cinder's breast, "Ah scared, Mama. Ah
hear em. They's comin ta gits me?"

Cinder only holds him tight, but opens her eyes to the
night.

Sheriff Tom and Deputy Hill walk through the smoke and
light of the flames. Deputy Hill follows behind, looking back
and forth at the dark faces that stand silently as he passes.

Katey stands on the porch, stands back in the shadows,
and watches the sheriff and the other man with the gun come
up through the smoke and into her dirt yard. She calls for her
God, but her lips do not move, only her breasts rise and fall
rapidly, then she speaks.

"What ya want here now? Billy ain't here. He ain't here,
Ah tell ya. What ya want here? Ya all go away from here."

"Where's that boy's mother at? Tell her ta get her ass out
here, ya hear me? Ah say, tell her ta get out here fore Ah
come in after her."

"She gone. She gone too. She ain't here."

"Ya lyin, get her out here."

"She gone, she leaves. She ain't comin backs here."

"Get out the way," Sheriff Tom shouts and bust into the
house.

Deputy Hill walks quietly through the dirt yard and around the back of the house and stands peering into the dark fields, then flicks his flashlight on and slowly waves its beam of light across the dark tall grass, then returns to the sheriff.

Sheriff Tom has come out of the house and stands on its sittin porch, snarling and cursing the night.

"God damn it. Damn it. Shit."

"Sheriff, Sheriff, they can't be far," Deputy Hill shouts ahead as he nears, "Ah reckon they out in that field, ain't noplace else they could be, she probably lit out in that field."

The sheriff becomes silent, then quickly says, "Go on back and get me Pete Grayson, tell him to get Chesty Collier and his boy Butch and get them dogs down here. Tell them ta bring some night-lights, and that's all, nobody else."

"You got it, Sheriff."

The night had deepened, the hours sunk deeper into darkness, where they stilled and just laid. Billy Lee had fallen asleep, has his head nestled in Cinder's warmth as she holds him close and watches the night. The fire's bright glow had faded into just a distant gleam of color against the dark grays and blacks, except for the calls of night bugs, the sudden flutter of bat wings, the squeal of death in the dark, it is quiet. Cinder's eyes are open, full of tears, slow tears that bubble, then burst and run down her cheek. Billy is warm against her, his slow breaths give a gentle rhythm to her thoughts. She thinks of Otis, thinks of maybe he will come now and take them out of the night, but she does not look for him, only thinks of him. She thinks of far-off places she has read about and seen in her picture books, brings them closer into her mind, puts herself there, and then the night brings her back. She is tired, tired of all that time has brung, tired of being what she has never felt, tired of feelings she feels

but does not understand. She thinks of death, not the death
of a faceless child, but a death of feeling, of being, death of
color, death of night and day, but mostly the death of time.
There was something she read, it was words about a river and
how it flows home to the sea. In her way she has never been
home.

She sees the lights swinging and flashing across the field,
but they just seem to be there, maybe been there all the time,
just swinging and swaying back and forth, not for her or of
her, just there in the distant dark of her mind. They are still
there, they won't go away, and she cannot turn from them; she
watches them sway back and forth in the night. She shudders
and feels the chill of a cold wind, then stills herself and sinks
deeper into her darkness and peers through the thick leaves
and branches of the bush. The lights still come. She turns
and looks behind her and into the swells of shifting grays and
blacks, then trembles and turns back to the lights. Her hand
moves quickly but gently, she places her hand over Billy's
mouth, then leans and whispers in his ear, "Billy, Billy, wake
up, baby."

The lights have sounds now, harsh muffled shouts and yells
that send their meanings into the night.

Cinder whispers frantically, "Wake up, Billy, wake up."

Billy moans, "Huh, huh."

"Wake up, Billy, wake up," Cinder whispers and shakes
him.

The lights sway and flicker back and forth and come closer.
Billy's eyes open, but close again, he begins to mumble.

"Mama, Mama, Ah cold. Ah wants ta go home."

"Wake up, Billy, wake up. Mama's here, wake up," Cinder
whispers quickly, then rises quietly in the dark.

Billy is cold and shivering, the darks of the night have no

color as he looks around. His mother's hand pulls him, her voice calls, "Come on, Billy."

She pulls him deeper into the bushes and away from the lights. Her own sounds, her quick panting breaths, the squishy sounds beneath her feet, the cracking of bush branches, are thunderous in her mind. When she cannot see, she reaches out and feels her way, moves thick bushes away, then slithers through the thickets with Billy by the hand. The bushes thin, and they can move faster, until the mud sucks their feet deep into its grip. Cinder keeps goin and whispering behind her, "Come on, Billy, come on." The sticky mud turns into cold running water that rushes through their legs, gets deeper, then swells to Cinder's waist and Billy's chest. She turns in the water, moves a different way, drags Billy on, but the water gets deeper and she stops.

"Mama, Mama."

"Hush, Billy. Hush, come on."

Cinder wades on through the dark rippling waters with Billy's hand over hers. The mud comes again, then soft grass they can run through, almost see its green, but it's the thick darkness ahead where she leads Billy to.

They are cold, their soggy clothes sag from them as they curl deeper into the dark. Cinder slows and looks back across the gray running waters of the Catfish, she cannot see the lights. She grabs Billy and pulls him close to her, then sinks down to the ground. Billy shakes in her arms and she quivers with him, but stares out into the night.

"Mama, Ah cold. Ah wants ta go home. They's comin ta git us?" Cinder does not answer him, only pulls him closer and pushes his face into her breast. Billy becomes quiet but still shivers as he falls back into his sleep. Cinder's thoughts drift into darkness, but there is color in her mind, colors of suns, of picture books, of Katey's face, of Otis in the nights. Color of yesterday, but none of tomorrow. She knows she has crossed the Catfish Creek, knows she must go further until she reaches the railroad tracks, but now she must rest.

The full face of darkness is midnight, and it hovers over Mississippi. It never smiles or laughs, shows its teeth, only its frown. If it weren't for its stars and its moon glowing, no one would ever look its way.

The lights come again, Cinder sighs and watches them bounce in the far night. They flicker, then seem to disappear, only leaving their glow, but now they appear again and just sway back and forth.

Cinder sighs, a deep sigh that ends with a quick whisper, "Billy, Billy, come on, wake up."

He is heavy in her arms, she tries to shake him, but he just slumps limply against her.

Coon dogs howl.

"Come on, Billy, come on."

Cinder is up now and dragging Billy into the bushes, her eyes like a cat's, piercing into the shadow forms before her.

Thick bushes move, but swing back at her.

Billy moans, yanks at her arm to slow.

Cold soggy logs trip up her feet, she stumbles.

Big bulging trees loom like creatures in the night.

Bush thorns bite.

Coon dogs howl.

Mud squishes around her feet.

Bushes are thinning.

Tall grass sways in the starlight.

Coon dogs howl.

Billy shouts, "Mama, Mama."

She stumbles and falls, rolls, and twist in the mud.

Can't find Billy's hand.

"Billy, Billy."

Her reach touches him.

Grabs him.

Drags him on.

Coon dogs howl.

"Billy, run."

Shouts and yells near.

Lights bouncing up and down.

Coon dogs howl.

"Billy, run, run."

Coon dogs howl.

"Mama, Mama, they git us."

Thorn bushes bite.

"Over there. See em, Sheriff?"

"Run, Billy, come on."

"See em? Over there, see em?"

Silence.

"They up in there, hear em? Right in there."

Night-lights sway and point into the darkness.

Dark bulging bushes flash gray, green, then go black again.

Coon dogs howl.

Water splashes.

"There they are, Sheriff."

Billy slows and trembles.

Cinder drags him on.

Lights flash in her darkness.

"Mama, Mama."

Coon dogs nip and sniff at her feet.

Lights come into her face.

She grabs Billy.

Hands reach and snatch at her.

She jerks away.

Her hair is grabbed, yanked, and held.

"Ah got her. Sheriff, got em."

Cinder pushes Billy away and screams, "RUN, BILLY, RUN, RUN, RUN, RUN, RUN. . . ."

Billy only runs back to Cinder and throws his arms around her waist.

Deputy Hill yells back over his shoulder, "Got em, Sheriff, got em over here."

Cinder falls to the ground, Deputy Hill lets her fall but holds on to her hair until the lights come out of the night and gather around them, he lets go of her hair and steps away.

Sheriff Tom steps forward, holds the night-light above, and shines its beam down onto Billy, but only sees the back of his head buried in his mother's breast. He reaches down and yanks on Billy's shoulder, jerks his face around, then steps back and mumbles something quietly.

"Huh, Sheriff?" Deputy Hill ask.

Sheriff Tom is silent, but waves his light over Cinder's face.

Pete Grayson comes up with his night-light and sways its light across the woman desperately holding her child and her face away from the lights.

"Damn, Sheriff, how old's this little nigger?" Pete Grayson asks.

The sheriff is silent, takes a few deep breaths, then mumbles, "Cecil, get that boy away from her, get him away."

Deputy Hill glances at Sheriff Tom, then moves towards Cinder and Billy.

Cries and screams tear into the night. Pete Grayson sees Cinder's face, and now he is silent.

Fred Sneed had come through the early-morning shadows on Front Street. Sundays were always slow getting started in Banes. Folks took their time getting things goin, streets were just about empty, but Fred had found some of his sittin buddies, J. J. Gates and Dexter Clayton already sitting out front of the Rosey Gray. They were all men in their seventies and eighties, chewed and spit tobacco as they talked. Fred Sneed looked like he might be the oldest, had deep wrinkles in his sunken face, but he still had a quick eye.

J. J. Gates and Dexter Clayton sat staring out into the middle of the empty street, their faces tight and their mouths tightly closed. Fred Sneed was still talkin.

"Ain't had nothin like this since that nigger went wild over in Greene. Can't have this, can't have it. Ah seen it spread, git one wild one, next thing ya know, got more of em. Ah tell ya, can't have it." Fred spit some tobacco juice from his mouth and looked up and down the empty street, then spoke again, "Ah tell ya, it ain't right, ya just can't have that around."

"Sheriff got em both down there now." J. J. Gates leaned back in his chair as he spoke.

"That ain't sheriffin business." Fred Sneed snapped his words.

"Nigger like that need hog-guttin," Dexter Clayton said through clenched teeth.

"Should have got it done last night," Fred Sneed spit and spoke.

"Sheriff chased em out of there," J. J. Gates spoke again.

"Should have burnt the whole damn nest out," Dexter Clayton snarled.

"It ain't right, what he done. Sheriff ought ta know better." Fred Sneed is fuming. He wipes the tobacco juice from his mouth, takes a deep sigh, and turns and looks up through the morning shadows to where the jail sits, then looks back down at his own shadow and says, "Just can't have this."

Over on Third Street, Doctor Henry P. Grey liked to take his Sundays slow and easy, specially if he had some of them Saturday-night baby deliverins, or some Dillion Street drunk to sew up. Sunday mornings for Doctor Grey was easy time. He set sipping on his coffee and watched the sunlight filter through the window, but yesterday was still on his mind.

Constance Grey was a northern woman, met her husband in Ohio when he was going to medical school, that was thirty-four years ago. Sunday mornings for her were special, she brings her coffee into her husband's office, where he sits, now, staring down at the forms on his desk. She sits in the chair by his desk, but he does not look up.

"Do you have to get that done now?"

"Mize well, before Tom gets here," Doc Grey answers without looking up.

"What's going to happen now, Henry?"

"I don't know."

"Those colored boys are just so young, Henry." Constance sighs and looks away.

Doctor Grey is silent, but starts to fill out the forms on his desk. He knows the sheriff will want the exact cause of Lori Pasko's death. He knows the sheriff will be by to talk to him, ask more questions than he can answer.

Constance looks back at her husband, sighs, and says, "This is so terrible, this whole thing is just awful. What's getting into people? They're so young too."

"That little girl is dead," Doctor Grey whispers.

"What do you think will happen to them, Henry?"

"There will be a trial."

"What will happen then?"

Doctor Grey is silent, and the room becomes quiet except for the scratchy sound of the pencil he is using to fill out Lori Pasko's coroner's report.

Over at the office of the Banes County *Times*, Harvey Jakes is having his morning coffee. His eyes are strained from being up most of the night, his tie is loose and hangs dangling from his neck, but his moves are quick as he leans back in his chair. His head jerks a little as the outer door rattles, he hopes it's who he thinks it might be.

The clicking taps of heels come through the outer office and Harvey Jakes smiles as Helen Marks comes into his office.

"Good morning, Mister Jakes. I thought I'd find you still here," Helen says with a smile on her face.

"Didn't expect to see you this morning, thought you'd be

getting ready for Sunday school," Harvey Jakes says, smiling and looking up at Helen Marks.

"Oh, Mister Jakes, I don't go to Sunday school," Helen teases.

"Glad you stopped by. I wanted to thank you."

"Thank me for what, Mister Jakes?"

"If it wasn't for you, I could not have done it."

"Oh, Mister Jakes, you don't have to thank me. I just wanted to see you get the extra out. I think it's great that you did it. Folks are really going to be talking. I bet they're going to be reading about this for hundreds of miles. I bet we won't get any returns. Everybody is going to buy a paper, just you wait and see," Helen says, then swishes around Harvey Jakes' desk and looks down at the paper sheets with the big headline print.

"Which one did you use, Mister Jakes?"

"I was going to use that top one, but the sheriff got that other boy last night, got him out behind the Patch, so I had to go with the 'KILLER CAPTURED' instead of 'KILLER ON THE LOOSE,' " Harvey says, gleaming.

"I like your lead, it's real good," Helen speaks softly as she reads the subheadline and first paragraph aloud: " 'Sheriff captures two colored in the brutal slaying of fifteen-year-old Lori Pasko who died of multiple knife wounds. . . .' " Helen stops and looks at Harvey, saying, "This is the biggest story in the whole state. This is good. This is going to be so exciting. . . ."

Harvey Jakes sits smiling, Helen ask if he wants another cup of coffee and takes his cup to the coffeepot. When she comes back to his desk, she sits on the corner of it and looks down at Harvey Jakes and says, "Mister Jakes, I've been out of Sunday school for years."

"I was only teasing, just teasing," Harvey says, blushing. Helen smiles.

Down at the end of Dillion Street and up the tracks some, Pete Grayson sits out on his back porch, he's been sitting there since first light of day, just looking out at the early-morning sky. Folks knew Pete Grayson for his distant ways and them coon dogs he could run; some folks remembered his young years, when he had them good looks, that straight black hair and them flashy blue eyes, remembered his Saturday-night days and that quick temper of his, but when he married Holly Pratt, that put an end to his Saturday-night days and ways. He had two boys, but they both moved out, now it's just him, Holly, and his nineteen-year-old daughter, Kelly.

Kelly Grayson has her daddy's looks, tall and slender with that jet-black hair and flashy blue eyes. When she opens up the back door and comes out on the porch, Pete Grayson looks up and smiles.

"Daddy, what ya doin out here? Mama wants to know if you want another cup of coffee," Kelly asks as she pushes the hair out of her eyes.

"No, honey," Pete Grayson says softly.

Kelly walks to the edge of the porch and stands stretching her arms and back, then sits down on the top steps and looks out into the morning.

It's quiet for a while, Kelly feels the sun come to her face, but mostly feels the silence on her back. She turns to her father.

"What's wrong, Daddy, why you so quiet?"

"Oh, just sittin, thinkin, thinkin how pretty you are," Pete Grayson says with a smile.

"Oh, Daddy, you ain't thinkin that. Why are you so quiet, what's wrong?"

Pete Grayson smiles, takes a deep sigh, and looks out past his daughter and into the faint greens of the distant fields and the blues of the sky.

"Mama says you went with the sheriff and helped get them niggers last night. Mama says if it wasn't for you them niggers would have got away. Said you caught them down past the Patch, had to chase them way out in that swampland back there. She says that nigger did the killin wasn't nothin but a boy. Says ya all had to chase him and his mama real far fore you could catch them."

Kelly's still talking, but Pete Grayson sighs and looks far, past where the sun comes from.

Sheriff Tom had slept on the cot in his office. Although he lived right around the corner from the jail with his wife and two daughters, he always stayed at the jail if he had prisoners in a homicide or some other serious crime. Most of the time, he leaves about midnight, after his Dillion Street drunks sobered up, or he just lock up and leave anyway.

The sheriff liked to take his Sundays doing as little as possible, maybe sneakin out the house and goin over on the other side of the blacktop to get some fishin in the river. He'd been sheriff in Banes for twenty-eight years and was the part-time deputy five years before he became sheriff. His full name was Thomas Jonathan Liebenguth, but folks just knew him as Sheriff Tom. He had his ways and was known for them. Had to do the things he did. Folks that didn't see, heard about the sheriff killing Zachary Higgins when the sheriff was still a deputy. Zachary Higgins went berserk and killed his wife and two children with an ax. The sheriff told Zachary Higgins he would kill him if he didn't put the ax down. Zachary Higgins laughed, and the sheriff shotgunned him. As time passed, folks became sure that the sheriff would do exactly what he said he was going to do. He had told old man Henry's boy Sam to stay out of his sight. Sam been out of jail and the state penitentiary past countin. He was down on Dillion Street, been drinkin all day and was all liquored up. He came at Sheriff Tom with a broken bottle, just like a mad dog. Sheriff shot him twice but he kept comin until the sheriff shot him again, then he went down. That's when folks say Sheriff Tom just went over to him, mumbled somethin, and shot him right in the head, then turned around and shot at them dogs that were barkin.

Sheriff Tom took his sheriffin seriously, didn't like nobody getting into his business, like to turn in a clean and orderly report. Folks had different things to say about Sheriff Tom, but everybody gave him his lead.

Sheriff Tom was up now, been up since dawn, and was sitting at his desk sipping coffee, waiting on Cecil Hill to come in, and scribbling on his notepad. He had the knife he found in Billy's pocket laying on the desk and was thinking about the evidence he had and the statements he'd get, then he backed away from his thoughts when he thought about bringing in Jenny Curran to identify the prisoner, the State would want that. The sheriff sighed, looked at the light coming through the window, then glanced at his watch. He knew he'd have to see Ely Hampton, the State's prosecuting attorney, and tell him he had a murder on his hands.

Downstairs, in the small cellblock, Gumpy sat in the corner of his cell. He wants to look up and look through the high window on the wall, but he does not want to move or make a sound. He thought he heard Billy crying in the night, when all the noise came, but he wasn't sure, he wasn't sure of anything. He looks down at the dark floor, then to the stripe of light hitting it from the window, and stares into the cracks and crevices the light shows in the cold cement floor. He closes his eyes and opens them again, the dark cement floor is still there, he turns and looks at the wall, and it is still there, he lowers his head and cries quietly.

At the other end of the cellblock, Billy is just wakening, he'd cried hisself to sleep, screamed into the night, called for Cinder to come get him, screamed so loud that Deputy Hill had to come down and shout at him until he stilled hisself, then he screamed again until sleep came and got him. Now he lays on the hard cot, pulling on his blanket. His eyes slowly open and it is just dark he sees, then the gray walls and the black thick bars. Then it is the night again, the lights coming to get him, then hands reaching for him and ripping him from his mother. Now he hears screams, hears the shouts and yells bashing into his ears and shaking his mind. He jumps up and looks around, jumps off the hard cot and runs to the thick bars and screams, "Mama ... MAMA ... MA-MA ... MAMA ... AH WANTS TA GO HOME.... MAMA, COME GITS ME.... MAMA ... MAMA ..."

Crows fly on Sunday too, their black wings flutter under the blue sky. The Patch Road goes a bit past LeRoy's, then it just seems to weaken into paths goin here and there, but only crows fly further today. To the side of the end of the road is the Patch church, First Star Baptist, been there since anyone can remember, old folks say it's been there since slavin days. It has its ways, folks whisper around it, speak quietly when they speak of it. Folks can see it from the road, see its pale-white color and that green waterland behind it. Folks sort of walk up to it kind of slow, keep their eyes down like they don't want to look up at that old dark wooden cross stuck high up over the door.

Reverend Sims sits back in his big chair behind the pulpit. His head is bowed and he's swaying with the Sunday music. Patch folks' hums and songs seem to float out from them and fill the air, deep slow sounds flow from shaded faces and gleaming white teeth, then the echoing notes of hums and songs leave a chord of silence.

Reverend Sims remains sitting with his head bowed, then he rises and slowly walks up to the dark wood pulpit and stands looking out over the shadowy faces. This is his time, his Sunday morning, this is when the world is his, no crows fly, no demons in the sky, he is in his house of the Lord.

He speaks.

"Ah got somethin."

Silence, then he speaks again.

His words flow slowly. "Ah got somethin ta say ta ya, got words for ya, got words Ah gots ta say."

He stops now, wipes the sweat from his forehead, then shakes his head before he begins again. "Ah got ta tell ya bad days are here. Bad days have come."

Now his voice is raspy, he twist and squeezes his words, gets all the pure feeling out of them. "We seen the fires, seen em in the night, heard our children cry. Some of us were beaten, some of us were . . . were . . . were dragged from our houses, dragged out into the night, dragged like animals. Whipped and beat, dragged while the fires burned with flames of evil. Flames of evil can burn your flesh right off your bones. The devil has his ways, he can come into the night and bring all his evil wit him.

"His fires can burn the flesh, but not the soul. His sticks can beat your back, but not your heart if it is of the Lord. The Bible say, the words of God tells ya . . . tells everybody . . . the Bible say, 'The enemy that sowed them is the devil; the harvest is the end of the world; ands the reapers . . .' Bible say the reapers, yes, '. . . the reapers will be God's angels.' Jesus is comin. Ain't no man of the earth can turn Him around. No man. He's comin and ain't no fires can burn Him. Ain't no sticks that can hurt him. Ain't no death that can end his life, ain't no evil that can stand up ta His love. Jesus. Jesus. Jesus will put the fires of evil out. Theys won't burn again."

Reverend Sims will go on now, his voice will crack through the hot sticky air, his hands will swing and draw pictures of his words he speaks, he will close his eyes and scream to the sky, but he will not stop talking about his God.

Patch dogs lay quiet in the morning shade, smoke still seeps from the burnt wood that was Gumpy's house.

Cinder lays beneath the light cover, her face flush against the feather-stuffed pillow, her eye closed, but she's not asleep. They had yanked and dragged her through the dark, jerked her back when she screamed and reached for Billy. She could hear Billy's screams, see him in the dark reaching for her and being yanked away by the big man that dragged him along the Catfish Creek until they reached the road where the bridge is, then the car came with its lights shining into the night. She'd lunged for Billy as they threw him in the car, but she was shoved away, then pushed to the ground, as the car disappeared into the dark. She just laid beside the road until the man who called her by her mother's name took her in his arms, talked to her in a way she never knew.

He brought her home, carried her up through the Patch paths, past the flames of Gumpy's house, until she was home and in Katey's care. Then he rubbed her hair, whispered something she could not hear, then vanished in the night. Katey took her into the house, laid her on the bed, and held her while she shook.

Now the sunlight nips at her eyes, she winces and buries her face deeper in the pillow. Katey has come to her again, sits at her side, and rubs her hand across her shoulders, but does not speak, does not say words, knowing nothing can be said.

Time cannot move from Cinder, she will not let it move, she reaches for it and grabs it and won't let it go, won't let it move, keeps asking what it will not tell, twisting her feelings beyond any words and asking again, but nothing comes to her mind, nothing, not even Katey's words now, that plead with her to put it in the hands of her God, "Take it ta Him," she's sayin, "take it to Him, child," but her words can't get into the dark corners of Cinder's skull, where her mind has curled into despair.

Jenny Curran is home. It is the first Sunday that she will not hurry up and eat, finagle her way out of her chores, then beg, sneak, or just run over her fields, and cross the hard road to Cousin Lori's house. She was afraid last night, everything moved in her darkness, shook her when it did, everything keeps happening again. Lori keeps falling to the ground with blood on her, Lori keeps looking up at her, she keeps seeing herself running across the field, keeps seeing the coffin being carried into Lori's house.

Jenny is not up yet, but her eyes are open. She does not want to close them again, look again at the faces in her night. Her mother's with her, has been with her all through the night. She sits on her bed and looks into her eyes and asks softly, "Jenny, Jenny, you want Mommy to get you some milk? You want some milk? Maybe some cookies too?"

Jenny does not come out of her stillness.

"Honey, you want Mommy to get anything for you?"

Jenny's eyes remain still and she is silent.

Her mother sighs and looks away and stares. She thinks of Lori and shudders, thinks it could have been Jenny and shakes, then turns back to Jenny, takes the cover down, and pulls her up into her arms.

Jenny's father's standing at the doorway, he is quiet, just stands and looks, then with a sigh he whispers, "How is she?"

"She's woke, she just ain't sayin anything, she won't talk," Jenny's mother whispers. "I don't know what to do, she shook all night, screamed in her sleep. I don't know what to do. She talked some yesterday, they said she talked to Sheriff Tom for a good while. I just don't know what to do." Jenny's mother's voice is fading, her father takes a deep breath, then whispers, "She'll be all right, she got to have her time, work it out her way."

Jenny's mother turns and looks at the sunlight coming through the window, then quietly and without words thanks her God for her child's life.

Ginger Pasko did not sleep at all, she would not leave Lori's side, Red Pasko sat with her.

Marcus Warden did more than he usually would, and did it with the grace of an angel of the night. He prepared Lori, embalmed her, washed the blood from her, combed her hair, then placed her in the coffin with the white dress her mother picked out. Then he put a little makeup on her cheeks and patted her face until it took the shape of peace, folded her hands beneath her breast. He had worked quietly, then presented Lori to her mother and father for approval. It was then that he sighed, bowed his head, and left without a sound or farewell.

David had made coffee for his mother and father and placed it in their reach. It is cold now, the cups are still full. It has not been touched.

When Deputy Hill came into the jail, he found Sheriff Tom still sitting at his desk scribbling.

"Mornin, Sheriff," Deputy Hill shouted with a grin on his face. Sheriff Tom remained silent.

"That boy quiet down after I left?" Deputy Hill asked.

Sheriff Tom nodded his head, then said, "He was hollerin again a while ago."

"Ya want me ta stand by while ya get some breakfast?" Deputy Hill asked.

Sheriff Tom kept scribbling and was silent for a moment before saying, "No, just go on over and get somethin to feed them boys. I want ta get that little one up here fore long."

There had been silence in the cellblock below, any moment seemed to linger. Billy sat in the far corner of his cell, his head was down and he just stared at the floor. A faint whisper comes, "Billy, Billy, ya be in there?"

Gumpy had whispered out to Billy, and now they whisper back and forth through the shaded cellblock.

"Hey, Gumpy, Gumpy."

"Huh, huh?" Gumpy's whisper is so faint that Billy can't hear and turns away from the bars and walks back to the end of his cell, then quickly turns around and scampers up to the bars again and yells, "Hey, Gumpy, Gumpy."

"Huh, Billy?"

"What ya doin?"

"Nothin."

"Ah hear em walkin. Ya hears me?" Billy whispers now.

Gumpy is quiet and tries to look out the cell bars to see if he can see Billy, then whispers, "They's comin ta git us, Ah hear em."

"Ya hear em, Gumpy, ya hear em comin?"

Gumpy does not answer, he is still and listening to every sound he hears. He shakes when he hears the clanging sound of the key going into the big steel door at the top of the steps.

Billy jumps back into the corner of his cell, his heart pounds with each heavy clumping footstep he hears.

Deputy Hill has his instructions on how to feed his prisoners, he is not to say anything to them, but make sure they do not feel free to talk amongst theirselves. He puts the plates of food down, then slowly walks the length of the walkway in front of the cells, stopping and staring at both Billy and Gumpy.

Then he shouts, "If I hear one goddamn sound comin out of your mouths, I'm gonna take my belt off and whip your black asses, ya hear me? Answer me when I'm talkin to ya, ya hear me?"

His words thunder through the cellblock, then he takes the plates of food and opens each cell and says, "Ya eat this, and ya eat it now. I be back down here in a minute and ya better have it gone." Then he leaves and goes back up the steps and clangs the big heavy door to.

Billy and Gumpy gulp their food down and sit quietly in their cells.

Sheriff Tom glances at his watch and mumbles over to Deputy Hill, "Get that little skinny nigger up here."

In a moment, Deputy Hill has Billy by the arm and drags him over to Sheriff Tom.

"Where ya want him, Sheriff?"

"Sit his ass down in the chair," Sheriff Tom mumbles without looking up from his desk pad.

Deputy Hill flings Billy into the chair and stands behind him.

It is silent. Billy sits hunched over in the back of the chair, his feet stick straight out, they cannot reach the floor.

Sheriff Tom does not look up but begins to mumble softly.

"What's ya name, boy, what they call ya?"

"Billy, Billy Lee," Billy whispers but keeps his eyes down and stares at the floorboards.

"Billy Lee, huh. Your name Billy Lee Turner?" the sheriff ask and looks up over his desk at Billy and keeps his eyes on his face.

Billy nods his head yes and squirms in the big chair.

"Where you live at, Billy Lee?"

"Wit my mama and Aunt Katey."

"What ya mama called?"

"My mama's Cinder," Billy whispers and begins to look up.

"How old you, boy?"

"Ah tens, but Ah be leven," Billy blurts out.

"When ya be eleven?"

"Ah be leven when its be Febueries. Ah be leven then."
Billy begins to look around.

"What ya do yesterday, boy, what'd ya do, huh?" Sheriff
Tom's voice rises and Billy lowers his eyes and looks back
down at the floor.

"Nothin, Ah ain't dids nothin. Ah wants ta go home."

"You ain't goin home, boy, I promise ya that," the sheriff
mumbles, then tries to grab his words back and starts again
with his questions.

"Where ya and Gumpy go yesterday?"

"We goes across wheres the train comes."

"What ya do then, huh? Where ya go then?"

"We ain't dids nothin."

"Did ya go up to that pond?"

Billy is silent, he lowers his head so low that Sheriff Tom
can only see the top of it.

"You can tell Sheriff Tom, Billy Lee, you can tell Sheriff
Tom. Come on, boy, tell me what happened. What ya do up
there? Ya bother anybody?"

"Ah ain't did nothin. We just be theres, me and Gumpy be
lookin for redbacks. We just doin that." Billy rushing his
words, his eyes have lifted and he quickly looks at the sheriff's face, then looks down again but keeps his words goin,
"We's ain't did nothin. Theys come and tries ta git us. They
big. Theys git me down and tries ta beat me up. Theys tries
ta keeps me down, but Ah gits up, Ah gits up."

"What ya do then, Billy Lee?" the sheriff asks quickly, and
glances up at Deputy Hill.

"She come and tries ta gits me again. She tries ta gits me
down again. She gonna tries and beats me up. Then Ah . . ."
Billy stops his words and squirms in his chair.

"What ya do then, huh? What ya do, Billy Lee?"

"Ah, Ah tells her ta leave me be."

"Did she leave ya be?"

"She tries and gits me again, Ah stuck her." Billy pouts.

"You stick her once, just one time, huh?"

Billy shakes his head yes, then begins to glance up at the wall.

"Where ya stick her at, boy?" the sheriff asks quickly.

"She comes and tries ta gits me."

"Where ya stick her at?"

"Ah stucks her where her titty be."

"Is this your knife? This your knife here?" The sheriff's voice rises to a harsh whisper, as he takes the knife off his desk and holds it up.

Billy does not look up, but sinks further down in his chair.

"God damn it, boy, look up here. Look up here at this knife you used to stab in that girl's heart, damn it, look up here, you hear me?" Sheriff Tom shouts and bangs his fist down on the top of his desk.

Billy's eyes fill with tears, he begins to quiver.

"Look up here, boy, damn it. This ain't no plaything here. Damn, ya done killed a girl. Look up here."

Billy keeps his head down, but flashes his eyes up at the knife, then shakes his head yes.

Sheriff Tom glances up at Deputy Hill and mumbles, "We got it. Take his ass back down and keep him quiet."

Billy is back in his cell now, and just sits staring at the light coming through the high windows, but the big white face of the sheriff is still in his mind. The moments go slow and only jump ahead when he hears the thumping footsteps from above, then he jerks and looks out through the thick black bars.

Gumpy sits with his hands squeezed tightly between his

legs. He wants to yell to Billy, ask him what they did to him, but he remains silent and only squeezes his hands tighter with his legs.

Sheriff Tom has left the office, told Deputy Hill that he be back in a couple hours, that he's goin home to get some breakfast. Deputy Hill sits with his feet up on the desk playing with a pencil as Harvey Jakes and Helen Marks come in.

Deputy Hill smiles and gets to his feet for Helen Marks, then looks at Harvey Jakes and says, "Sheriff ain't here, Mister Jakes. Can I help you with somethin?"

"Well, I was hoping to talk to the sheriff," Harvey Jakes says. "I guess you know we have the biggest story in the state here now. Folks are going to want to know how you caught them, and what's going to happen to them."

"Sheriff ain't here now, Mister Jakes. He ought ta be back about noon. He just went on home to get some breakfast," Deputy Hill says with a smile for Helen Marks.

"You got them right downstairs here?" Helen Marks asks with an excited look on her face.

"Yes ma'am, right downstairs, got both of them there."

"What do they look like, they mean-lookin?"

"Nope, just two little niggers," Deputy Hill says with a grin.

"Can I look at them, would you take me down? I wouldn't want to just go by myself, can you take me down? Would that be all right?" Helen asks with the biggest smile she has.

Deputy Hill is silent for a moment. Harvey Jakes says quickly, "I think it would be all right. I'd like to see them myself, see what they look like so I can describe them better in the paper. Miss Marks is my assistant. I think it should be all right."

"Ah don't know, Mister Jakes. Ah don't know if it's fit

for womenfolks. Ah think the sheriff ought to be the one ya ask."

Helen Marks says quickly and coaxing, "I'd be all right with you there with me, Cecil."

"Well, Ah don't know. Ah don't know what the sheriff would say."

"I just want to take a peek at them, see what they look like, Cecil. It will just take a little minute."

"Well, all right, just a peek. Ya can't stay long and ya can't say nothin to them, can't ask them no questions," Deputy Hill says and whisk around to get his keys.

Billy and Gumpy both jump as they hear the big steel door opening. Gumpy can only hear the sounds of feet coming down the steps, but Billy can see Deputy Hill's legs from his bars, then the swishing dress-covered legs of Helen Marks. He backs away from the bars and gets in the corner and holds hisself still. The footsteps come closer, but it's the ones that click that make the sound he listens for.

Gumpy does not move, he stays back, sitting on his cot playing with his hands and fingers.

Billy looks up from his corner when the clicking heels come close, then he stares up at the tall white woman with the long yellow hair looking in at him.

"Which one's this? He's a skinny one, look at him," Helen says with a smile and a tug on Deputy Hill's arm.

"This the one that did it, this is that Billy Lee Turner one."

"Look at him, Mister Jakes, he gives me the creeps."

Gumpy hears the footsteps coming, but does not look up, turns even further towards the wall.

"Turn around here, nigger, turn around," Deputy Hill shouts.

Gumpy turns but does not look up. Harvey Jakes asks,

"How old's this one? He looks a little bigger than the other one."

"This one's says he twelve. Sheriff got him first."

"He sure is an ugly little thing. Just look at him." Helen makes a face with her words.

"What did he do? Did he hurt the girl too?" Harvey Jakes asks.

"Sheriff can give ya the details. Come on, we better get back up," Deputy Hill whispers and leads them to the steps, but then stops as Helen goes back down to Billy's cell, saying over her shoulder, "I just want to see this one again."

Billy hears the clicking heels coming again, turns, and looks up.

Helen Marks looks in, she leans closer to the cell bars and tilts her head some to get a better look at Billy.

Billy keeps his eyes on hers, then turns away as he sees the smile on her face fade into a snarl. "Watcha lookin at, nigger?" Helen whispers and stares at Billy, then turns away smiling and saying, "You think they'll put him in that electric chair?"

Constance Grey went to the door and saw Sheriff Tom's big silhouette through the screen.

"Come on in, Tom, Henry thought you might be by. Can I get you a nice cold drink, how bout some ice tea?"

"No ma'am, just had my dinner. Thank you, though," Sheriff Tom says as he takes his hat off and tucks it under his arm.

"Come on in, Tom," Doctor Grey calls from his office.

The sheriff comes into Doc Grey's office and takes that chair right next to his desk.

"You going to get any fishin in today?" Doctor Grey asks, smiling.

"Oh, hell, Henry, I don't think so," the sheriff says with a sigh.

"I figured you might be by. Got it all done for you."

"What's it look like Henry? Anything I didn't see?"

"I don't think so, Tom. Looks like that blade just got far enough up in her to nip at the aorta, that accounts for all that blood. She was bleedin pretty bad, I don't think anything could have helped her. It can happen like that sometimes. That blade just got up in there at the wrong spot. God, what's this world coming to?" Doctor Grey sighs, looks up at Sheriff Tom, and waits for his next question.

"Was she bothered any, Henry?" the sheriff asks as if just routinely.

"No, Tom, I'm certain of that."

"I didn't think so, just had ta ask."

"Heard you got the other boy last night."

"Yep, got him out behind the Patch there. His mama had him back out there in the bushes, took a couple hours to flush em out. That mama of his put up one hell of a fuss. Ah tell ya, she was like a wildcat."

"How old's that boy you got down there?"

"Damn, Henry, he ain't but ten years old."

"What the hell happened? What got into him? What did he do a fool thing like that for?"

"Far as I can tell, Henry, the boys were wadin in that pond down there, girls went down to chase em out, got to fightin, and he gets that knife out. It's a shame, but that's murder, don't make a difference how old he is. I tell you now, that boy ain't got the slightest idea what he done. Other one's just a little older, twelve, he ran before the knifin." The sheriff took a deep sigh.

Doctor Grey sits quietly and waits to see if the sheriff wants to talk some more. He knows the sheriff is closed-mouthed about things, but comes to him to talk. Doc Grey had a way with Sheriff Tom, shared a little corn taste every once in a while, got some fishin in together when they could.

"Had me some hotheads last night, Frank Ottum and that bunch. I come on down in the Patch, already burnt that one boy's house down, whipped a few niggers. You know that big nigger Jake? I think he busted a few of them up. That's one nigger I hope stays tame," the sheriff finished with a small laugh.

"You think there'll be more?" Doc Grey asks.

"More what? Knifins or burnins?"

"More of both."

"I don't know, Henry. Ain't no tellin when niggers go wild, but this thing here different. Far as the burnins go, I can't be down that Patch all the time. Folks goin ta be plenty upset seein that little girl dead, and that little nigger walkin around breathin, Ah tell ya that."

When the sheriff got back to the jail, Deputy Hill told him of Harvey Jakes' and Helen Marks' visit, then figured he better tell him about taking them down to see the prisoners. The sheriff just shrugged his shoulders and said, "Wait till tomorrow, we'll probably have a line outside. Mize well get used to it till they're outta here. Just don't let any unofficial folks down in there, and don't let nobody ask em any questions, no talkin at all."

Mid-Sundays in Banes had their ways, folks that went were coming back from church, other folks took to talking over fences. Most folks were surprised to see that EXTRA paper on their doorstep and picked it up real quick. Reading and talking buzzed from one side of town to the other. Churchgoin folks started cooking something extra, planned on getting together and taking some food out to the Paskos.

Up on Front Street, Fred Sneed read his paper aloud to his sittin buddies. In the Rosey Gray, folks peeked over one another's shoulder, trying to see the big headlines. Marcus Warden took his paper in the back of his burial shop, poured hisself another glass of bourbon, and read slowly.

Down on Dillion Street, at Jack's place, some folks were just starting their day, but they tried to get the red out of their eyes to read the fine print too. At the end of Dillion Street, Pete Grayson listened while his daughter, Kelly, read the paper aloud and gasped at the ugly details. He kept his head down.

At the far end of the other side of town, Judge A. J. Harper took his paper into his office at home, closed the door, and read it by the window light, then read it again, sighed, then scowled his face tightly.

Banes sidewalks and streets were never full or busy on Sundays. Folks just came and went in fews. Most folks you could tell a block away who it was by the way they walked. Strangers would stick out right away, but today most folks walked like strangers, strides were quickened or slowed. Shorty would usually show up bright and early on Sundays, hang around out back of places, waitin on someone to call his name, have somethin for him to do, then he bounce up to them with a smile, do their biddin, and get a nickel or some cooked food.

Shorty had come to town the back way, kept in the back of them places down on Dillion Street, came around some of the fences. Dogs didn't bark long, they all knew Shorty and just barked once, then wagged their tail. Shorty got up to Front Street and got behind the Rosey Gray. He sits there now with his busted lip parched up in a smile, he has not heard his name called.

Out on the blacktop at the Moskin High Hotel, Wilbur Braxton sits with his daughter Megan, since his wife died he takes his Sunday dinners at the hotel. Megan was away most of the year at school, studying political science at Chatham College in Pittsburgh, she wants to be an attorney like her father. It was Megan that saw the big-headlined paper one of the other guests was reading and went to get one. She has not said a word since she started reading, just keeps brushing her sandy-colored hair from her eyes. Her father will not interrupt her until she is through, that is his way, he is a very patient man, known for his patient ways.

"This is awful, Daddy, just awful," Megan whispers over the page.

Wilbur Braxton remains silent.

"Daddy, that poor girl, she was only fifteen, and the Nigras that did it were just young boys. One was just ten years old. I declare, this is just terrible," Megan says as she folds the paper.

"What is so terrible?" Wilbur Braxton asks.

"It's just terrible," Megan says, then catches herself and her father's look and says, "According to these allegations, 'Two Negro boys, ages ten and eleven, are being held in the Banes County jail for the stabbing death of Lori Pasko, age fifteen, of Banes County. Both of the Negroes are believed to have lived in the Patch area.' "

Wilbur Braxton nods and then ask to see the paper, reaches into his vest pocket and gets his bifocals out, and slowly puts them on, and begins to read.

"Daddy," Megan says quickly, then catches her thought and remains quiet, knowing that her father has told her: Always give someone the time they need to understand what the allegations are, and they understand the point of your questions you are asking. Then, if they do not answer promptly and precisely, you can assume that they are not about to tell the truth, and not merely that they are not informed.

Megan watches her father read, watches for the expression to change on his face. It did not. It remains impassive, as it always does when a jury enters a courtroom.

Wilbur Braxton was raised in the outskirts of Banes County, near the Greene County line. He'd spent his early law years in Jackson, only returning to Banes when his father died and left the estate in his name. Rufus Braxton was a cotton giant, with more cotton fields than most folks ever seen. Wilbur Braxton took over the business as a family tradition.

Wilbur Braxton had married late, he was forty-five when he married Francine Hemper of Jackson, she had just turned twenty-three. Francine died at Megan's birth, that was twenty-one years ago. Now, Wilbur Braxton, years show in his thin, tall structure, showed his dark hair as dark cold gray, showed his face with wide wrinkles of time, but it was the coughing spells that seemed to mark his time, left him shaking with embarrassment and took the words from his mouth sometimes, cut his wind.

For her father's sake, Megan Braxton tries not to show outwardly concern for her father's failing health, but it is only for her father's sake, not hers.

"Appears to be an interesting case. Lots of unanswered questions, of course," Wilbur Braxton says softly as he folds the paper.

"You won't get it, Daddy, will you?"

"I certainly hope not. It could extend me beyond my capabilities."

Megan was silent, she wanted to let her father know he was still capable, but she did not want to encourage him.

"Of course, if I'm called upon, I'll have no choice, matter of principle. I'm quite sure Ed Jamison isn't going to want to touch it. You know he has plans to run against Merritt Elrod come fall. Don't think he has a chance at it, but he's a young man and won't see it that way. Now, Jack Davenport is up and coming, has a good record, and Carl Herbert's a fine fellow too, he might be available, but taking this case against Ely Hampton is not going to be an easy task. Ely is a tough prosecutor." Wilbur Braxton kept his soft tone as he spoke. Megan had put her head down to avoid his eyes and hide the concern on her face, then she changed the subject quickly.

"Daddy, I think Stepper is coming up lame. He's been favoring his right front like it's a little sore. Do you think Josh put the shoes on too tight? I'm a little worried, with the show coming up." Megan brought her father's attention to her words. She had that way with him.

"Well, let's don't jump to any conclusions. We'll take a look at him when we get back, maybe get Josh to pull that shoe and soak that foot some, keep him in the stall and see how he goes in the morning," Wilbur Braxton said, sighed, glanced out the window, and kept his stare.

Morning lights started coming on before dawn, Banes folks were getting ready for Monday, coffeepots perked and old coon dogs stretched. By the time first light came, folks were into their day. In an hour or so, Banes streets got busy, most folks headin down to the saw-yard, other folks having one last cup of coffee before opening their street shops. Pickin fields were fillin up, black backs were already bent, old mules that weren't ready to move yet just didn't want to pull them wagons, put up with folks, had field men hollerin, "Hee, hee, hee, gitty awn. Gitty awn here. Hee, git on up here."

Banes was surging into its day when Sheriff Tom walked up the courthouse steps. His walk was brisk, he kept his eyes straight ahead, didn't turn to them calls of "Hey, Sheriff, what ya goin ta do with them niggers ya got? Sheriff Tom, hear ya got them killin niggers down there." He walked into the shade of the courthouse hallways and into the solictor's office and filed his papers with the clerk, then asked, "Ely in yet?" Mrs. Caroline Hempfield nodded yes to Sheriff Tom, and he went straight into Ely Hampton's office.

Ely Hampton was a short stern-faced man, not known for his humor, had straight ways and quick wit, always seemed to be doin something, talked real fast when he spoke, then shut up just as fast when he wanted answers. He was fifty-three, still had all his hair except for the little round bald spot on the back of his head, kept his face clean-shaved, got a shave over Hanner's cuttin shop every morning, sometimes twice a day.

"Whatcha got for me, Tom?" Ely Hampton asks quickly and without looking up from his deskwork.

"Got two confessions, one witness, murder weapon," the sheriff is saying.

"What's the motive?" Ely Hampton interrupts Sheriff Tom.

"Trespassin, lookin for trouble, lookin to bother folks," the sheriff says and takes a seat.

"They bother the girls any? That other girl, was she bothered?" Ely asks before the sheriff even set good.

"Don't think so. Don't see it, got some bite marks and scratches on the Pasko girl, but don't see she was bothered."

"Let's get them arraigned on first degree." Ely Hampton spoke quickly, then looked out the window for an instant and turned back to the sheriff saying, "What's the ages of those boys, Tom?"

"The one did the knifin, ten. That other boy says he's twelve," the sheriff grunted, then rubbed the back of his neck.

"Uh huh," Ely Hampton says, "let's get them over here and get them arraigned. Let's say one o'clock on the nose."

Banes had not said much to Shorty, hadn't even asked him about his busted lip, just had him doin his chores like always. Norma Purvis been calling him for an hour or so, had sent for him, needed some packages picked up on Front Street. She was a little irritated when he finally bounced up to her back door.

"I declare, where on earth you been? I been fetchin for ya for the last hour. Now, you take this money and give it to Mister Macky, he'll know what it's for, and then you get on back here with those things, go on now." Norma Purvis shooed Shorty away.

Fred Sneed and more of his sittin buddies, them old Banes men that didn't come out much, came out today, all of them had their talk going and kept glancing down to the jail when they wern't pointing and pulling on them newspapers they still had.

Banes men down at the saw-yard were moving things around a little quicker, and throwing words over their shoulders. Everybody'd seen the paper and most of them knew Red Pasko, some of them were distant kin.

Carmella Dean was a striking woman of twenty-eight, but had hard ways, she worked down at the beauty shop on Dillion Street, but took her lunch up at the Rosey Gray. She was talking to Rhoda Lucas while she was doing her hair.

"I tell ya what, I don't care how young them niggers are, they go and do somethin like this, kill that poor girl, they need killin themselves. I don't want that kind around me at all, killin folks like that. I think they ought to just take em on out somewhere, get it done with. Havin em around just keeps remindin ya what they done," Carmella was saying as she finished up and got ready to go up to the Rosey Gray for lunch.

Harvey Jakes had wasted no time in getting over to see Ely Hampton and comes running back into his office to get his camera. Helen Marks whipped around in her chair and asked, "What's goin on, Mister Jakes?"

"Ely says the sheriff is bringing them boys over to the courthouse, and I want to get a picture of them in time for page one," Harvey Jakes answers quickly, reaching for his big Speed Graphic camera. Helen Marks sits patiently before sayin, "I sure would like to see that."

Caroline Hempfield takes her lunch a little early, told Ely Hampton she would be back in time for the arraignment. On her way to the Rosey Gray, everybody she talked to she told, "Sheriff's bringing them out about ten to one. Bringin em right over to the courthouse. Charge is gonna be murder in the first degree."

High noon did not bring sunlight into Billy's cell, just strengthened the harsh shadows. Deputy Hill had made his feeding rounds, now it is whispering time. Billy had learned from the sound of the footsteps above his head when someone was coming down into the cellblock, knew as soon as the big door rattled, someone was comin.

Gumpy had begun to move around some in his cell, looked forward to the hot sandwiches and soup. He could not see Billy, only his hand if he stuck it out far enough through the bars. They whispered most of the hours now, until the footsteps above got close to the door, then they'd dash for the corners of their cells.

They are whispering now.

"Hey, Gumpy, Gumpy."

"Huh?"

"Ya think theys lets us go?"

Gumpy does not answer, only thinks of Billy's question. Billy waits a moment, then calls again, "Hey, Gumpy, ya think our mamas come git us, ya think that? Ya think we's can go fore dark time?"

Gumpy remains silent.

"Hey, Gumpy, maybe we's can sneaks out? Maybe we's can sneaks up and gits out the window. We's can waits till they's sleepin."

"We can'ts do thats, Billy, theys gots bars on them windows. Can't ya see em?"

Billy is silent for a moment, then whispers, "Ah wants ta go home."

Gumpy whispers back, "Ah wants ta go home too. Ah don't likes bein in heres. Ah tells ya they git us." Gumpy's whispers jolt, his eyes pop wide open, then he scoots back into the corner of his cell.

Billy leans against the cell bars, listens, then gets back in his shadowed corner.

The big heavy door clanks open, the thump of footsteps coming down the steps begins.

Deputy Hill comes into the shadows, stands silently looking back and forth through the cell block, then turns and goes to Gumpy's cell and takes the key and inserts it into the lock, swings the door open, and shouts, "Get out here, get out here right now, ya hear me?"

Gumpy shrinks back into the corner. He is trembling and begins to cry when Deputy Hill shouts again, "Damn ya, boy, get your ass over here now, fore Ah come in there and get ya."

Gumpy throws his eyes up into Deputy Hill's face and keeps them there as he eases off his cot and inches his way to the big white man.

"Get over here now, damn it," Deputy Hill shouts as he begins to lose patience and knows Sheriff Tom is waiting for him upstairs. He reaches over and grabs Gumpy's shoulder and jerks him out of the cell, yanks him around, and then grabs his arms and pulls them behind his back. Gumpy's cries become screams and he begins to squirm and wiggle away screaming, "Ah didn't do nothin. Ah wants ta go home. Lets me go home, mister. Lets me go home."

"Shut up, god damn it. Ya don't shut up, Ah take my belt to ya, boy. Shut up," Deputy Hill yells as he takes his handcuffs and puts them around Gumpy's wrists and squeezes them to their last notch. He yanks Gumpy around and out into the walkway and shouts, "Ya stand here, right here. Ya move one step and Ah come back here and beat your ass for ya."

Billy has squirmed deeper into the shadows of his cell, but the whites of his eyes cannot hide from Deputy Hill. He is already shaking when Deputy Hill puts the key into his cell door, shouting, "Get your ass over here now, boy."

Front Street had a face that was not smiling, it was like an old face, a stone face that did not warm up with the high hot sun. Banes folks stood watching, waiting, whispering to one another in their wait. The Rosey Gray had emptied, Fred Sneed and his sittin buddies stood, Caroline Hempfield scooted through the crowd and went back to the courthouse, Carmella Dean moved to the edge of the sidewalk. Harvey

Jakes stood on the courthouse steps, Helen Marks was by his side. Shorty bounced up the street and went into Macky's store lookin for Mister Macky.

The jailhouse door opened and Sheriff Tom stepped out into the harsh sunlight, looked around, and mumbled something back inside, then stepped slowly down the steps and waited. Deputy Hill pushed the two dark skinny shadowed colored figures into the harsh sunlight. He had each one by the back of their necks, pushing and steering them down the steps.

"There they are. . . . Here they come. . . . Look at em. . . . Damn niggers . . ." the mumbles began.

James Maben and Andrew Miller moved from the sidewalk and started towards the night-colored boys, others on the sidewalk followed.

"Goddamn niggers . . . Look at em . . ." the mumbles were becoming shouts and snarls.

Carmella Dean yells out, "Ya ought ta kill em right now, Sheriff."

Sheriff Tom kept his pace.

Deputy Hill pushed Gumpy and Billy faster, but kept his eyes on the approaching crowd.

Melody Curran, a distant relative to the Paskos, breaks from the crowd and runs up behind Deputy Hill screaming, "You killed Lori, you rotten black bastards. You bastards. You killed my cousin."

Gumpy shakes and squeezes his eyes closed.

Billy tries to look around, but flinches from the shouts and yells.

Sheriff Tom keeps his stride.

Fred Sneed yells, "Hey, Sheriff, Sheriff, Ah got a rope over here for ya. That's what ya need for em."

Deputy Hill looks behind him and sees the crowd approaching.

Carmella Dean spits once, then runs up closer and spits again in Gumpy's face.

Deputy Hill pushes Gumpy and Billy away from the crowd.

"Little black bastards. Nigger animals," shouts come closer.

Tears seep through Gumpy's closed eyes.

Billy leans closer to Deputy Hill.

James Maben picks up a rock and throws it at Gumpy's back.

Gumpy jerks, his eyes flash open, and he screams.

Deputy Hill pushes him on.

Sheriff Tom quickens his pace.

Melody Curran spits on Billy, then grabs at his arm.

Deputy Hill shouts, "Ya all get back, get away, ya hear."

Andrew Miller gets Gumpy's arm and snatches him away from Deputy Hill.

Gumpy is flung to the ground.

Melody Curran kicks at his face.

Andrew Miller kicks at his side.

Carmella Dean brings her heel down onto his back.

Gumpy's face scrapes against the street.

Sheriff Tom turns around.

Deputy Hill reaches for Gumpy.

James Maben snatches Billy from Deputy Hill.

Billy screams as he is thrown to the ground.

Sheriff Tom shouts, "Get outta here, god damn it, get on out of here."

Billy is kicked and dragged.

Deputy Hill pushes James Maben away, shouting, "Get outta here, Jimmy."

Shouts fill the street, "Get em. . . . Get that one. . . . Niggers. . . ."

Melody Curran gets her foot on Billy's face and squashes it. Billy screams.

Sheriff Tom barrels into the crowd and pushes folks back. Deputy Hill gets Gumpy and grabs for Billy.

Helen Marks stands on the courthouse steps, smiling. She watches the crowd surge onto the nigger prisoners and the sheriff pushing and tossing them back.

Harvey Jakes runs and climbs up on the courthouse fence, gets his Speed Graphic camera up to his face, he clicks the shutter, the flash burst, he smiles.

Sheriff Tom's face is rigid and twisted, his shouts are like growls, his hands grab and push like claws.

Deputy Hill pulls the two screaming prisoners under his arms.

Ely Hampton looks out the window and shakes his head.

Caroline Hempfield looks out the same window and says, "That's just awful."

Helen Marks is still smiling with excitement as Sheriff Tom and Deputy Hill drag Billy and Gumpy up the courthouse steps.

Billy's eyes are glaring, he catches a glimpse of Helen Marks and keeps staring until he is yanked away.

Deputy Hill pushes the courthouse door open and steers Billy and Gumpy through.

Sheriff Tom stands at the door and faces the crowd, they back off slowly. Then he turns and follows Deputy Hill and his two prisoners into the dimly lit courthouse corridor.

Ely Hampton comes out of his office and rushes up to Sheriff Tom, saying, "Looks like you had a little trouble gettin them over here, Tom."

Sheriff Tom's breath is heavy. "Goddamn hotheads, I'm gonna knock the livin hell out of em."

"Get em on in here and let's get this over with." Ely Hampton speaks quickly and then glances over at Billy and Gumpy and says, "Cecil, take em on in there, get em cleaned up some, can't have em lookin like that," and points to the rest room.

"Can't take them in there, these is niggers, Mister Hampton."

"We ain't got time to run em downstairs, just take em on in," Ely Hampton says quickly.

Inside Courtroom C, a small hearing room at the end of the first-floor corridor, clerks and secretaries are buzzing around the open door. Banes County Commissioner Austin Hunt stands inside, puffing and chewing on his two-inch cigar. Banes Mayor Devin Marshall stands beside Austin Hunt. Both were talkative men, but they stood silent amidst the babble in the hearing room and corridors. Matthew Brady, the chief county clerk, stands behind the large table with all his legal forms for the arraignment spread out before him. Harvey Jakes comes rushing into the room all red-faced and his camera swinging, saying, "Folks got a little nasty out there." Helen Marks follows him through the door.

The corridor chatter stills into a gasping sound. Sheriff Tom and Deputy Hill push Billy and Gumpy through the crowd and up to the table. Their faces are battered and bruised, their arms are still held behind their backs, their screams now muffled into whimpers, each battered head is hung low. They stare at the floor where their tears fall.

Matthew Brady looks down at Billy and Gumpy, then glances over to Austin Hunt. Austin Hunt nods his head and

Matthew Brady turns back to Billy and Gumpy, stands quietly for a moment, then says, "Quiet, please."

Room C becomes silent except for the whimpers of its prisoners. Matthew Brady begins, his voice is in a singsong rhythm.

"Let the record show that on August twenty-three of our year nineteen hundred and thirty-seven, Billy Lee Turner, age ten, and Roy Thomas, age twelve, both residents of Banes County, Mississippi, are being arraigned and charged with murder in the first degree, in the stabbing to death of Lori Pasko, age fifteen, also a resident of Banes County, Mississippi."

Billy and Gumpy stare at the floor, they only hear the sounds of words battering inside their battered heads.

"Billy Lee Turner and Roy Thomas, you are to remain incarcerated in the Banes County jail until a hearin date can be set. If you do not have legal counsel, one will be appointed by the court to represent you."

Out on Front Street, Fred Sneed had set back down but Melody Curran was still strutting back and forth. She'd just turned twenty and had that Pasko-Curran red hair, but it was her face that lit with fire when she saw the nigger standing with the packages in his arms and the smile on his face.

"Whatcha smilin at, nigger?" Melody Curran yells.

Shorty had heard so many screams and shouts of "nigger" that he did not realize the woman was yelling at him until he saw her eyes glaring at him, then he knew. He'd stood and watched the crowd surge on Billy and Gumpy, had watched Sheriff Tom bust into the crowd and push and beat folks back. He was waitin to see if they would do it again when the sheriff brought Billy and Gumpy back out, but now he turns and starts up the sidewalk and back to Norma Purvis' with her packages.

Shorty's bounce is swift until he hears the sound of footsteps rushing up behind him and the shouts coming closer of "Get his ass, come here, ya little runt nigger." He turns and looks over his shoulder, then stumbles before he can break into a run. He darts into the alleyway, between Macky's store and the Rosey Gray, and rushes through its shade, but the shouts and footsteps follow. Norma Purvis' packages are falling from his arms, he slows to pick them up, then feels the hands reaching and swinging at him. He is caught and dragged out behind the Rosey Gray.

The crowd gathers.

Andrew Miller kicks at Shorty's back and side.

James Maben beats Shorty with a board he's picked up.

No one is trying to stop Melody Curran from kickin the smile off Shorty's face.

Patch children went screaming to their mamas when they saw Shorty coming up the road. They told their mamas, "Mister Shorty all beats up, gots bloods all on him." Patch mamas got to calling them children. Folks inside them shacks got to coming out to see what was going on. Shorty wasn't talking to nobody. Folks seeing him from a distance would have thought he was drunk, done had too much of that stuff LeRoy got, but him coming the wrong way and not having a smile on his face told folks that staggering walk was a hurtin walk.

Reverend Sims' God said to him, "Go git Big Jake and gits Shorty off that road."

Della Robinson had heard all that fussing and came out on her sittin porch. When she saw Reverend Sims and Big Jake holding Shorty up and all that blood on Shorty, she shook her head and went on back in the house.

Reverend Sims and Big Jake got Shorty up in that shack of his, and Big Jake got Shorty to talking some. Shorty told Big Jake what Big Jake already knew, he told Big Jake, "Ah wasn't doin nothin. They come and beats me. Ah wasn't doin nothin to nobody." Reverend Sims got to praying to his God and asking Him for some understanding he was needing.

Shorty's words couldn't get too far before they turned into moans. Big Jake shook his head and left. Reverend Sims got Shorty cleaned up and told him, "Ah be back in a bit. Ah bring ya some soup to sip on."

Patch children sat on their sittin porches. Their mamas told them, "Ya's stay up here, don'ts be goin no further." They watched Reverend Sims come down from Mister Shorty, then some watched when Reverend Sims stopped, looked over to the pile of burnt wood where Gumpy used to live, then they watched him look up to where Billy Lee be livin, then they knew to look away when Reverend Sims got to just shaking his head.

A Patch mama called out, "How he be doin, Reverend?" Reverend Sims looked her way and said, "They beats him bad, but it don't look likes they break anything. He be fine in some time."

Reverend Sims kept walking as the Patch mamas followed him. "It ain't right, Reverend, it ain't right what they's doin."

Reverend Sims was still looking around for that understanding he had asked his God for.

Big Jake went on down LeRoy's, had to get on out of Shorty's shack.

"What ya say?" LeRoy asked.

Big Jake had sat down at LeRoy's counter and had his head

lowered as he said, "Ah ain't seen nothin like it, the ways theys went on and beats that man."

Quickly LeRoy asked, "What he do up there?"

Big Jake just kept lookin down in that dirty countertop of LeRoy's and saying, "Ah ain't seen nothin like it. Shorty looked like somethin the dogs got at. Ah had to come on out of there."

"What he do?" LeRoy asked again.

Big Jake said, "Ya know Shorty don't be botherin folks. He up there doin their doings and theys just did him like thats."

LeRoy poured a drink and drunk it real fast, then said, "Folks ought ta stay out of there. Let them white folks simmer down. Next thing ya know, theys git that hangin on theys mind. Git ta wants ta kills them a nigger. Ah knows one thing, it ain't goin ta be me. Ah blows the first one's head off that come back up in here."

Big Jake wasn't saying anything for a while. LeRoy had poured him a drink, but Big Jake wasn't drinking either. LeRoy got quiet too.

Big Jake sighed and finally said what he was thinking about. "That Cinder's boy ain't nothin but a child, can't be twelve yet. Miss Katey sayin he ain't but ten."

LeRoy gave a quick laugh, then said, "That ain't makin no nevermind ta them. A nigger a nigger. Shorty always be down here wit that talk about them good folks up there. He did nothin but be a nigger. Ya sees what he gits."

Big Jake kept his head down. LeRoy was quiet for a while, then said, "Ah tells ya, Ah kills some of thems if they tries and comes back up in here."

Big Jake told LeRoy he was goin on home, he'd see him later.

Patch folks was wishing the sun would stay. Some of them

got to looking both ways, watching the sun going one way and that dark coming the other. Reverend Sims had gone back up to Shorty's and sat with him for a while until night came. Before he left Shorty, he asked if Shorty wanted that lantern of his on. Shorty said no.

Katey sat with Cinder, but she sat alone with her thoughts. Her face was buried in her hands, her eyes were closed to the night. She had put her hands to the sky, tried to touch a reason for days gone by. She had stopped reaching now, the reason she sought will not come to her and she cannot reach any further beyond herself. Cinder will not let her come any closer to her. She had whispered to Cinder, "Child, ya gots to sleep. Jesus is goin ta bring that boy home," but her words had only faded into the dark.

Cinder was no longer Cinder, only a soul seeking death, dying, then being yanked alive by white hands in the night snatching her baby.

Patch dogs lay still, but did not sleep.

The dirt is still soft on Lori's grave. Flower petals glisten with early-morning dew. First light peeped through the window at Ginger Pasko; she sat alone in her emptiness. Days gone by have not left her yet, taunting habits won't go away. An innocent thought is lingering, it leaves a faint smile on Ginger's face. Lori is crying and tugging at her dress. Ginger can pick her up and hold her. Lori's tears will go away.

Red Pasko is awake, he lays staring into the early light. He is thinking of days he has never spoken of. Days when men screamed as they died, the sounds of the guns never stopped. He could hear the screams and guns again. His peace and joy are shattered.

Banes streets were filling up with sunlight and people.

Some folks were getting their morning coffee in the Rosey Gray and looking at them pictures Harvey Jakes put in his newspaper. "Oh, look—there's me." Carmella Dean was pointing to herself in the picture. Clyde Bruce was pointing and saying, "Ah almost had that one there." Other fingers pointed and poked at the pictures of Billy and Gumpy being dragged through the jeering crowd.

Sheriff Tom had not seen the paper; he had slept at the jail and now sat waiting for Deputy Hill to come. When the door opened he did not look up, he knew the sound of the footsteps were Cecil Hill's.

"Mornin, Sheriff."

Sheriff Tom nodded his head.

"Ya see the paper, Sheriff? It got a big picture right on the front page. Got ya and me right in there too."

Sheriff Tom shook his head no and mumbled something that Deputy Hill did not hear.

"Ah got us one."

The sheriff looked up.

"Everybody talkin about it, Sheriff."

Sheriff Tom took the paper and looked at the picture, said nothing, then gave the paper back to Deputy Hill.

"What ya think, Sheriff?"

Sheriff Tom shrugged his shoulders and looked away.

Billy slept and played with his dreams, but his dreams ran away and hid. He was awake and just staring at the gray walls of his cell. He had heard the footsteps above and cringed with every sound. Slowly he eased himself to the edge of his cell and whispered through the bars.

"Hey, Gumpy, hey, Gumpy, ya's be woke, huh?"

Gumpy was sitting quietly on the far end of his cot. He had wanted to call for Billy but he was fearful of his own sound. Billy's whisper came again, and Gumpy slowly rose from his cot and tiptoed to the bars and whispered, "Billy, ya's woke too."

Billy whispered back, "What's ya doin?"

Gumpy stood silently, but his eyes flashed about the empty walkway in front of his cell.

Billy called again, "What's ya doin, huh?"

"Ah ain't doin nothin," Gumpy answered.

"Ya hearim walkin too?" Billy asked.

Gumpy was silent, then whispered quickly, "Ah hearim. They's comin."

Billy's eyes widened; he stood silently until he heard the big clank of the upper door, then he scooted back to the corner of his cell. Heavy footsteps slowly descended the steps, then Deputy Hill's voice shattered the stillness. "Ya all better be up and standin front and center when Ah get down there."

Billy stood still and Gumpy's eyes fell to the floor.

"Ah told ya, ya better be standin front and center when Ah come down here," Deputy Hill shouted as he reached the bottom of the steps and did not see his two prisoners.

Billy stood in the corner of his cell and lowered his head when Deputy Hill came and stood in front of his bars. "Git over here," Deputy Hill shouted.

Billy slowly looked up.

Deputy Hill shouted, "Ya hear me comin down these steps, Ah want ya standin right up front here, where Ah can see ya. Ya hear me? When Ah come down here Ah want ta see ya. Now, git over here right now."

Billy moved slowly towards the big man.

Deputy Hill shouted again, "Boy, ya better learn how ta move, now git over here."

Billy hastened his steps, but lowered his eyes. Deputy Hill

shouted, "Now, next time Ah come down here, Ah want ya standin right here so Ah can see ya."

Billy stood quietly.

Deputy Hill's voice lowered as he handed Billy the plate of food and said, "Now, ya got ten minutes to eat this, and ya better eat everything." Billy took the plate of food and carried it back to his cot while Deputy Hill called Gumpy front and center.

Banes folks were doing what they do. Some of them were even calling Shorty's name and waiting for him to come. The noon hour was nearing. Mrs. Purvis was busy shopping in Mister Macky's store. Pete Grayson's wife, Holly, was there too. After a few short words of greeting, Mrs. Purvis was saying, "Isn't it just awful. Ah just couldn't believe something like that could happen around here." Holly Grayson sighed and agreed, then said, "My Pete helped the sheriff catch them. Ah just can't believe they were so young." Mrs. Purvis spoke quickly. "Some of them just have that in them. Ya just have to watch all of them."

Ely Hampton was in Judge A. J. Harper's chambers. The judge had told him to stop on by. They had been talking for a while, but now they both sat quietly. Judge Harper is holding on to a thought and turning it over in his mind. Ely Hampton waits patiently. Finally the judge says, "I'll notify Wilbur Braxton, he'll do well." Ely Hampton gave a quick nod of his head, then said, "Judge, the state will be filing first degree." Judge Harper sat quietly for a moment, then said slowly, "Folks will want it that way."

Harvey Jakes had a big smile on his face all day. He had sold all the papers he put out. Helen Marks was smiling too; Harvey Jakes had asked her to lunch. They would be going over to the Rosey Gray.

Banes' noon hour was near, folks were slowing down their pace. Courthouse clerks were putting their things away. Matthew Brady always carried his lunch to work, and on nice days looked forward to having it outside on one of them benches. Fred Sneed still had the paper in his hands. He had been sitting all morning with his sitting buddies, J. J. Gates and Dexter Clayton. They sat quietly, sometimes the only sound would be the *piff* of a quick spit of tobacco.

Some of Banes' young people were milling about. Lisa Alo and her sister Janet had just crossed the street before they had to walk in front of "them spittin old men." They were both in their early teens and knew Lori from school, but they had never known anyone that was murdered before. Lisa and Janet could still see Lori in their minds and tried to remember the last time they saw her alive, but each one cringed when the thought occurred that it could have been them, then cold chills made them shiver. Janet had just shown Lisa the picture in the paper, they hated the two niggers they saw.

The noon hour was passing. Matthew Brady was folding up the paper bag he carried his lunch in. Mrs. Purvis was walking past the courthouse with her groceries in her arms. Harvey Jakes and Helen Marks were just about to leave the Rosey Gray. Lisa and Janet Alo slowed their stride and stared down the street. Fred Sneed spit his tobacco out, stood, and stared.

No wind blew in the streets of Banes, but Cinder's hair flowed and the skirt of her long yellow dress snapped with every step she took. Katey followed; she had pleaded with Cinder, "Child, ya can'ts go in there with them white folks actin like that."

Cinder had only looked at her and turned away.

Katey had said, "It ain't time ta goes in there yets. Ya gotta gives it time."

Cinder said, "I want ta see Billy Lee."

Patch folks watched Cinder as she weaved down through the shacks and started up the broken Patch Road. Patch mamas got up from their sitting porches and got to calling to one another, "Where she thinks she goin? Ah told ya that woman ain't right." Patch children stopped their play and watched. Katey was still pleading, shaking her head, but following.

Dillion Street folks saw Cinder cross the tracks, they stared, some followed from a distance. They sorta figured that fast-walkin woman was lookin for trouble and was goin ta find it.

Mrs. Purvis did not recognize the Nigra women she saw coming, but she could not take her eyes from her.

Pete Grayson was coming out of Hanner's cuttin shop and saw the woman he calls by her mother's name pass. He must follow.

Lisa Alo and her sister Janet's steps slowed to a stop. Janet looked away from the Indian colored woman, but Lisa had to see the woman's face.

"Look a-here. Look what's goin over ta the jail," Fred Sneed called over his shoulder to J. J. Gates and Dexter Clayton.

Deputy Hill had fed his two prisoners lunch and was now having his own lunch with Sheriff Tom. He quickly turned his head to the monotonous tapping on the door, then looked back at Sheriff Tom. The sheriff kept eating, mumbled something, then gave Deputy Hill a look that said, "Damn, Cecil, see who that is."

Sheriff Tom heard Cecil saying, "What do ya want here?," then he heard him call out, "Sheriff, it's that Billy Lee's mama."

Sheriff Tom sighed, then shouted, "Just tell her ta git on away from here, that boy ain't allowed no visitors."

Sheriff heard Deputy Hill saying, "Git out of here, ain't no visitors allowed here," then the door slamming.

A grin was on Deputy Hill's face as he started back into the office; it quickly disappeared when the monotonous knocking came again. "Damn," he shouted and went back to the door. Sheriff Tom rubbed the back of his neck as he heard the shouts of "Now, Ah told ya, now. Ya git on out of here. Now, git goin."

The door was slammed again, but before the slamming sound left Sheriff Tom's ear the monotonous knock came again. Deputy Hill shouted, "Damn bitch!" The sheriff was up and roared, "Ah take care of this."

The monotonous knock stopped when the sheriff jerked the door away from it. Cinder stood staring up into his eyes. He shouted at her, "Ya better git out of here."

Cinder just stared. Katey stood behind her saying, "She just come to see her childs. Can'ts she just see him? She just wantin ta see if he all right."

Sheriff Tom spoke to Katey, "He can't have no visitors gittin him all riled up. Now, ya all go on, now." Cinder spoke, "I want ta see Billy Lee."

Sheriff Tom shouted in Cinder's face, "Ah said git on out of here."

"I want ta see Billy Lee."

"Ah told ya ta git out of here. Ya hear me?"

Cinder stared, her eyes glowed the color of her burning soul.

"Git on now. Git out of here."

"I want ta see Billy Lee."

Sheriff Tom's shouts blew into the streets. Those folks that weren't looking stared. Lisa Alo and her sister edged closer. Mrs. Purvis stood still with her groceries in her arms. Matthew Brady was about to go back into the courthouse, but he didn't.

Cinder would not move. Katey softly pleaded to her, "Come, child."

The skin on Sheriff Tom's face tightened to the bone, but Cinder would not take her eyes from it. Someone watching shouted, "That must be one of em niggers' mamas."

Harvey Jakes and Helen Marks had just come out of the Rosey Gray and heard Sheriff Tom's shouting. Harvey Jakes got his notebook out and started across the street; Helen Marks followed. Clyde Bruce started across the street, yelling ahead, "Git outta here, nigger." Carmella Dean's face twisted into a bitter glare; she followed Clyde Bruce into the street.

Katey felt the eyes of evil on her back, glanced over her shoulder, and saw what she felt. Quickly she tugged on Cinder's arm, but Cinder would not turn. Sheriff Tom shouted, "Look, ya ain't doin nothin but startin trouble. Got enough of it. Now, git out of here."

Cinder's eyes narrowed as she hissed, "I want ta see Billy Lee."

Sheriff Tom's gut heaved.

Clyde Bruce yelled, "Ya nigger bitch!"

Carmella Dean was close enough to spit.

Deputy Hill darts around Sheriff Tom and tries to hold the crowd back.

Quickly the sheriff shouts at Cinder, "Git the hell outta here, now!"

Cinder raises her head and calls to the jail's big gray walls, "Billy Lee, Billy Lee. It's Mama. It's Mama, Billy Lee."

Carmella Dean spits.

"Billy Lee. Billy Lee. It's Mama, Billy Lee."

A faint cry that seemed to be an echo curling from deep beneath the jail's big gray walls stilled the moment. "Mama, Mama!" Billy Lee was calling from his cell.

Cinder's eyes opened wide. All of her tears just fell on out. "Billy . . . Billy . . . Billy," she cried to the big gray walls.

"Git her outta here," Sheriff Tom shouted to Katey.

Carmella Dean reached for Cinder's hair. Deputy Hill pulled her away.

Clyde Bruce raised his fist. Pete Grayson grabbed his arm and shoved him aside.

Katey recognized the man Cinder did not know, the man that called Cinder by her mother's name. "Alma, Alma," Pete Grayson called to Cinder. Cinder turned to the sound of her mother's name. Pete Grayson neared Cinder, saying, "Alma, let Katey take ya home now. Sheriff Tom will let ya see that boy of yours in a few days." Cinder looked into Pete Grayson's eyes and she became still, only her tears continued to flow. She knew the voice from the dark night, it was the voice of the man who carried her home. Pete Grayson spoke softly again, "Alma, Katey goin ta take ya home now. Ya go with her."

Katey stared at Pete Grayson too, she knew what Cinder could only feel but not know, then she reached for Cinder. A moment lingered, then Cinder turned with Katey's touch. The crowd watched Cinder walk away.

The faint cry of "Mama, Mama," tried to follow Cinder, but it could only go so far.

10

Evening was falling: the gray-shadowed corner of Billy's cell was turning black. He had called after Cinder, then cried the day away. Deputy Hill could not shut him up. Sheriff Tom said, "Let the boy be." Gumpy had whispered to Billy, but Billy didn't whisper back.

The big door clanked. Gumpy jumped to his feet and stood at the front of his cell, then whispered, "Billy. Billy, they's comin. They's goin ta yells if ya ain't ups." Billy turned his face to the corner.

The heavy footsteps grew louder as they neared. Sheriff Tom looked at Gumpy standing at the front of his cell, but said nothing to him. Billy heard the footsteps approaching, but he did not turn to their sound. Sheriff Tom came to Billy's cell and stood looking in. Billy did not look up. "Ya still cryin, boy?" Sheriff Tom asked. Billy was silent and kept his head down.

"Look up here, boy. Ya still cryin?"

Billy kept his head down.

Sheriff Tom was silent for a moment, then said, "Ya supposed ta be a big boy, ain't ya?"

Billy took a quick peek at the big man that keeps him, then put his head back down.

"Ya supposed ta be a big boy. Big boys don't cry. Look up here when Um talkin ta ya."

Billy turned to his dark corner, but he heard the heavy footsteps go away, then the clanging sound of Gumpy's cell door being opened. The footsteps neared again. Billy looked up and saw Gumpy. Sheriff Tom opened Billy's cell and put Gumpy in, then said, "Now, if Ah hear any more cryin comin out of here, Um goin ta take my belt to the both of ya all. Ya hear me?," then closed Billy's cell and left.

Blackbirds had flown high in the long sky. The waters of the Catfish had rippled, but the old broken Patch Road just lay somber as it always did. Cinder and Katey had walked silently on the road until Cinder slowed her stride and asked, "Who is he?" Katey lowered her head and walked in silence. Cinder asked again, "Aunt Katey, who is he? Why does he call me Alma?"

Katey sighed, but kept silent. Cinder had quietly walked on until she slowed her steps and turned to Katey. "Why won't ya tell me?"

Katey kept her head down and looked at the little pebbles and patches of green weeds growing in the ruts of the road, then slowly she said, "Some things ain't ta be sayin of."

"I want ta know."

"It's who ya feel it is, child. Now, lets it be."

Cinder walked on in silence.

Whispering and watching nights went by. Some Patch folks kept them nights-lights down low, they didn't want anyone seein them at all. Some of them other Patch folks got to sneaking into the dark, had to get down LeRoy's and get them a couple sips. Lucy Mae been down LeRoy's since before the sun went down. When she ain't drinkin she's cryin about Gumpy. LeRoy was just listenin, Lucy Mae was sayin, "Ya ain't feelin whats Um feelin. Ain't nobody's feelin whats Um feelin. Theys come takes my baby. He ain'ts dids nothin. Ah ain'ts gots nothin and theys burns my house too. Gumpy ain't dids nothin. Thats Billy Lee's just like that mama he got, like her and that daddy he had. Ah knows somethin was goins ta happen with that woman and them ways she gots." LeRoy was glad to see Wesley Hall coming in and scooted away from Lucy Mae real quick.

Big Jake was sitting over in the corner and hadn't said much to anybody after he told LeRoy to just give him a bottle. When LeRoy had asked him how Shorty was doin, he said, "Ah was up there some. He still just layin. Reverend be givin him some foods ta eats, but he ain't eatins much. Shorty ain'ts gots that Shorty in hims."

LeRoy was still talking to Wesley Hall when Aldon Fleming come in. LeRoy shouted, "Where ya been keepin yaself? Ah thoughts Sheriff done drags ya off too." Aldon Fleming was a big skinny boy that lived up there behind Della Robinson. He shouted back to LeRoy, "Shit, Ah seen that shit comin. Soon's Ah hear abouts they's lookin for some niggers for killin some white's child, Ah say lets me keeps my ass outs theys way." LeRoy shouted something back. Lucy Mae kept talking about Gumpy. Big Jake didn't say anything to anyone. The night stayed awhile, then slowly moved on.

Morning came and children played, even played around the burnt pile of what was Gumpy's house. The younger ones ran with smiles on their faces and eyes that were so big they saw an innocent time, until Patch dogs barked. Then smiles would run away and big brown eyes would only look for mamas.

Older children played too; they had a new game. They chanted, "Runs and hides, and if ya's found, Sheriff Tom's comin, gonna takes ya ta towns."

Old Patch folks just kept sitting. Reverend Sims told them everything would be all right. Them real old ones that done seen some time, knew them days Mister Pete talked about, had sad eyes. Netty Lou Moore remembered things Mister Pete forgot. She could remember before them Yankee soldiers come; she could remember belonging to them Hatchers too. She told Reverend Sims, "Ah done seens some bad times. Wasn't nothin be back here. Ya has ta wades in the Catfish ta gits back in here. Ah remembers. Its was right ups there. Ya sees where the roads be now. Its was right theres they comes. Never forgits. Theys come and gits that boy. Ah remembers. They comes and gits him. His name was Elijah, that's what his name was. Theys come down on thems horses and gits that boy. Says he was stealin and doin too much lookin at thats white man's woman he was doin for. Theys comes down here on thems horses and drags thats boy. He sayin he ain'ts dids it, but theys drags him away and theys hang him rights down theres where the roads goes over the Catfish. Thems were bad times. Ya all can'ts remember. Wern'ts born yets. Thems were bad times. They's comin agins."

Patch dogs barked.

The big gray car slowed and then stopped down on the red Patch Road. Patch mamas called their children. Patch folks stilled their doings. Wilbur Braxton eased his car door open, then stood and put his hand up to shield his eyes from the sun as he looked up into the Patch shacks.

Katey watched the white man from a distance, then shuddered and frantically whispered to Cinder, "Child, child, he comin heres. He's comin ups here. Lords, what's this man wants?"

Cinder came to the door and watched the man weave up the yard path. She stared to see his eyes, but she could not.

"Good day, ma'am. My name is Wilbur Braxton. I'm looking for Cinder Turner," he said as he looked at Katey.

Katey asked quickly, "What ya wantin with her?"

Cinder stood in the doorway and kept her eyes on the man.

"I am an attorney." Wilbur Braxton is speaking softly. "I have been appointed by the court to defend her son, Billy. I just like to talk with her for a moment."

"What that mean?" Katey was saying before Cinder stepped out of the shade of the doorway and came out onto the porch. "I'm Cinder Turner," she said sharply.

Wilbur Braxton looked up at Cinder and was silent for a moment, then said, "Mrs. Turner, I'm Wilbur Braxton. I'm a lawyer. I've been appointed by the court to defend your son, Billy. I like to ask you a few questions if I may."

Slowly, Cinder comes down from the porch. Her eyes are tired and strained, her long black hair hangs loosely over her shoulders, her copper skin seems tarnished from the rough days and the claws of the night. She stood silently for a moment and looked in Wilbur Braxton's eyes before asking, "What's going ta happen ta him?"

"I'm going to do my best, Mrs. Turner. I'll do my best to see that Billy gets a fair trial. I know you want him home. I'll do my best."

"When can I see him?"

"I'll inquire with the sheriff. I'm quite sure you will be able to see him soon."

Megan Braxton was sitting in her father's car. She had insisted on coming to the Patch with him. Some of the children have come near the car, but when she looks at them they run away. She can see up into the shacks and shanties and watches her father gesturing to the Indian-looking colored woman with the long black hair. She sees the others, the living souls of the shacks and shanties, standing silently watching her father. She has always seen them from a distance. They are the pickers of the fields. They are there when the sun comes, their chants give music in the day, then they leave with the last light of day. Her father is coming back down the weaving path; he has left the Indian-looking colored woman standing erect in the shambles of despair around her.

Agony chased Wilbur Braxton, and time ran away from him. He had filed motion after motion before Judge A. J. Harper and argued in the hot, sticky hearing room.

"My God, Your Honor," he had pleaded, "this boy is only ten years old. Obviously he is not an adult, or even close to his manhood. The fact is, Billy Lee Turner is just a child. This case must be tried in juvenile court. Trying this child in an adult court is a clear violation of his rights. Certainly he cannot be judged by a jury of his peers. And for the State of Mississippi to seek a first-degree murder indictment and to be seeking the death penalty for a ten-year-old boy, a child, is simply immoral. Your Honor, the defense asks that the charge of first-degree murder be lessened to a charge of involuntary manslaughter and be tried in the appropriate court of judiciary prudence."

Judge A. J. Harper had sat and listened.

Ely Hampton jumped to his feet and spoke quickly. "Your Honor, this boy here didn't steal some candy or break a window and run off. This here boy, regardless of his age, committed murder in the first degree. Murder is no child's crime. And let me remind the defense that there is a little white child lying out there in her grave. The State has the obligation and the will to prosecute as the law prescribes. Ah might add here that the law is very clear. If a minor commits an adult crime, and murder in and by its nature is an adult offense, that minor, regardless of age, is to be tried as an adult, and punished accordingly if convicted. This here boy is no child when he kills."

Judge Harper had leaned back in his chair and was pondering his thoughts. Wilbur Braxton quickly said, "Your Honor," then sighed and shook his head and continued, "The State's mere mention of imposing a death sentence on a ten-year-old Negro boy will send thunderous shock waves through this entire nation. Mississippi will be scorned by every state in this country."

Judge Harper jerked his head up, his eyes steadied on Wilbur Braxton's face. His words came quickly. "This is Mississippi. That little girl was Mississippi. This Nigra, this Billy Lee Turner, is Mississippi, and Mississippi will attend ta its own affairs as it sees fit. I hope I have made myself clear."

Wilbur Braxton stood silently shaking his head.

Judge Harper cleared his throat, then gave his ruling: "The State of Mississippi will hear the case of *Mississippi* versus *Billy Lee Turner* in the Banes County District Court. Due to the nature of these here charges, this boy will be tried as an adult. However, the jury will be charged with finding the degree of this boy's guilt. I am setting the date for this trial ta be held November first of this year. This court is adjourned."

Harvey Jakes' paper told Banes folks the news of Judge Harper's ruling. An uneasy calm with ripples of waiting settled over Banes.

Sheriff Tom had kept Gumpy in Billy's cell and gave them a checkers set. He told Deputy Hill, "That will keep em quiet."

When the nights fell, the long hours of darkness seemed not to go away. Billy and Gumpy would cuddle together beneath their blanket. The long silent hours would sometimes bring whispers in the nights: "Billy, Billy, ya's sleep?"

Silence.

"Billy, ya sleep?"

"Whats?"

"Ya sleepin? Ya think it's be mornin soon?"

"Ah don'ts know."

Gumpy was warm to Billy in the nights. Long days may see smiles in a shaded cell, or hear laughter. Billy was getting real good with his checkers.

"Ah gots ya, Gumpy!"

"Ya ain't wins, Billy."

"Ah gots ya."

"Ya can't move there."

"Can so."

"Ya can'ts, Billy."

"Ah wins. Ah gots ya agin."

"Ah quit, Billy."

"Let's play agins."

"No, Billy. Ah ain'ts playin wits ya."

A day passed, and another night. It was morning. Deputy Hill had already fed his prisoners. Billy and Gumpy had the checkers set out when the big door clanked. "They's comin,"

Gumpy hissed a whisper. Deputy Hill rushed down the steps and came to the front of the cell where Billy and Gumpy stood. He spoke quickly as he unlocked the cell door. "Come on, boy, ya got ya hearin taday." Gumpy's eyes flashed with fear. Billy watched as the big man led Gumpy from the cell and up the steps.

The morning was slow without Gumpy, but before its hours passed the big door cranked, and Billy's eyes smiled as Deputy Hill brought Gumpy back down the steps. "Wheres theys take ya?" Billy quickly asked as soon as Deputy Hill went away.

"Theys takes me over there agins."

"Theys beat ya ups?"

"No. Theys ain't came, theys leave me be."

"Whats they do?"

"Theys says Um goins ta a camps wits other boys. Ah goes theres tomorrows. Theys comin and gits me then."

"Theys say Um goin wit ya?"

"No, they ain't says that. They say my mama can comes and sees me at the camps."

Billy was silent for a moment, then asked, "How comes Ah can'ts go wit ya and my mama comes see me at the camps?"

"Theys says Ah runs and ain'ts kill that girl. They says ya makes her die. They says Ah was goods. Ah runs away, so Ah can goes ta the camps and my mama can sees me."

Gumpy wanted to play checkers, but Billy did not want to. Gumpy wanted to talk all day, but Billy just looked away. The black hours came; Gumpy slept. Billy called for dreams, but they did not come.

Deputy Hill came before the noon hour. Billy heard him coming as Gumpy jumped up saying, "Theys come gits me now." Deputy Hill unlocked the cell door and took Gumpy out. Billy said, "Ah sees ya, Gumpy."

"Ah sees ya, Billy."

Deputy Hill took Gumpy up the steps. Billy watched him go away, but Gumpy did not look back.

Wilbur Braxton had come to tell Cinder of Judge Harper's ruling. He had told her he'd done his best to keep Billy's trial in the children's court, but the judge said no.

Cinder was silent for a long time. Wilbur Braxton waited patiently for her to speak. Patch folks stood watching from their sittin porches. They could see the white man standing in the yard and had watched him lower his head. They could see Cinder standing with her head held high, but she stood silently. Only Wilbur Braxton heard her say, "They want ta kill him, don't they?" He answered quickly, but his words stumbled and fell. "Oh no, Mrs. Turner, they . . . well, it's going to be a trial by jury. They will see that Billy is just a child and did not intend to hurt the Pasko girl."

Cinder had looked into his eyes as she listened to the sound of his words, and when he finished speaking it was only the pounding of her heart she could hear.

"Mrs. Turner, this is nineteen thirty-seven. There are rights that will protect Billy from an unfair trial. The jury will see he is just a child and certainly did not mean to harm anyone. We have a good case to show that Billy was beat up and was only afraid. He did not intend to hurt that girl."

Katey had stood on the porch listening. She could not hear all the words Wilbur Braxton was saying, but the far skies seemed to darken with every word she could hear.

Patch dogs barked and chased Wilbur Braxton's car as he drove away. Reverend Sims walked up the path to where Cinder stood, but Cinder turned from him and went away. Katey stood still. Reverend Sims asked, "What dids the man say?" Katey shook her head and shrugged her shoulders as she started to talk. "Lord, Ah don'ts knows. They's ta tries Billy. They's goin ta puts him up there likes a man."

Patch folks could feel the feelings and got words from them. Patch mamas shook their heads and told one another, "Somethin's wrong."

Big Jake told LeRoy. LeRoy poured a drink and started talking about different things and then he started telling Big Jake, "Ya knows Ah don'ts wants a lot. Ah knows they ain't a lot ta gits anyway. Ah just wants me a little space likes Ah have. Ya knows them folks gots it all, gots all of Mississippi ya can see, gots this whole country too. Theys gots all the say-so. Gots the last words, can do what theys want. Theys gots it all and wants ta keep on takin. Ah makes up my minds a long time ago. Ah ain't give em nothin else. That's why Ah stays down here, Ah ain't givin em none of me."

Big Jake stayed down LeRoy's all day and into the night. When he left, the moon was showing its full face; the shacks and shanties of the Patch stood stark in the bright night. Big Jake turned from the Patch Road and started up the weaving paths. When he looked up, his steps slowed, and he lowered his head and walked in a reverence of silence.

Cinder was on her porch; she stood leaning against the porch post with her head down. She did not see Big Jake.

11

Mississippi's summer of nineteen thirty-seven faded. Days cooled as long nights chilled. The lights of the Patch flickered again, fires would burn soon. Patch children played in the day. Patch mamas talked in the night, but the stillness that had come in the summer lingered. Patch folks would only whisper about Billy Lee. Their whispers asked questions of days nearing.

Cinder could be seen. Patch folks would watch her, but did not stare, and never looked into her passing eyes. She had become frail with days gone by. Reverend Sims would go to her. Sometimes she let him near and listened to his words, some days Reverend Sims knew to leave her be. He'd tell Katey, "Ya just tell her she gots ta believe."

November's first day came on a Monday. Harvey Jakes put

out an extra paper; its headline read "BOY KILLER COMES TO TRIAL." Monday's sun had not risen yet. The courthouse was dark and empty; just the sound of its night could be heard, the shifting of its wood, the scratching of its mice. Sheriff Tom and Deputy Hill led their prisoner through the dark, chilling street. Billy was shivering and flinched from every dog's bark.

First light was first to come. County clerks of habit followed; they wiggled their keys in courthouse doors. Folks from afar who had heard the news had traveled in the night. Banes folks who lived around the corner began making their way.

Patch folks, just a few, were coming on the broken Patch Road. Cinder walked through the shadows the night had left on the road, Katey was by her side. Reverend Sims followed: he had his slavin Bible. His God had told him, "Walk with Cinder this day." Big Jake was coming too, he had told LeRoy, "Ah gots ta go."

Courtroom A was ready, and its bench seats were filling up. Quick whispers burst through the hum of restless chatter: "There he is." "That's him." Sheriff Tom was bringing Billy through the side door. Fingers still pointed at Billy as he slouched down in the big hard chair next to Wilbur Braxton. In the far rear of the courtroom, where coloreds can sit, Cinder sits high in her seat, but she cannot see her child.

Judge Harper called his court to order, then told Matthew Brady to seat the jury. Twelve faces of men filed into their seats. Cinder could see them; she tried to see into their eyes, but the faces were too far away.

Billy kept his head down as Ely Hampton told the jury, "Ah represent the State of Mississippi. Ah represent you, the people of Mississippi. Together we represent Lori Pasko here today." Then his words began to whip and snap at the air: "A knife in the hand of that vicious Nigra boy slashed the life away from Lori. She was just fifteen. . . ."

Billy cringed from the wind of the shouting man's words.

Cinder looked straight into the storm of sounds, tried to see where her child be.

Reverend Sims watched Wilbur Braxton rise and try to turn a wind gone wild. Big Jake listened and nodded his head yes as Wilbur Braxton told Banes folks, "Billy Lee Turner is just ten years old, just a child. A frightened child. What happened at that pond was a tragedy. A tragedy. Not a vicious crime."

Red Pasko's eyes burned red with fire.

Silence was a witness as Wilbur Braxton's words stilled and he took his seat.

Banes folks saw Sheriff Tom take the witness seat and heard him tell Ely Hampton, "Ah found that little girl layin in her mama's bed. She was dead when Ah got there."

Cinder saw the man that keeps her child from her; she did not listen to what he had to say.

Jenny Curran shook when Ely Hampton called her name. She has on her light-blue dress, the one she only wears to church and wore to Lori's funeral. Her long red hair is tied in a pony tail and gently hangs down on her back. Her hand is trembling on Matthew Brady's Bible. Her words are faint when she says, "Ah do."

Banes folks leaned up in their seats as Jenny took her time and told them about the day at the pond when Lori died. Billy kept his head down, but looked up when he heard the red-haired girl crying out, "That's him. That's him right there. That's the nigger that stuck Lori. That's him. He killed Lori. Ah saw him. He stuck her and made her die. Ah hate ya, nigger."

Ginger Pasko sat quietly; tears seeped from her silence.

Banes folks watched Ely Hampton strut and peck before the jury until the noon hour came. Judge Harper looked at his watch, cleared his throat, then announced, "We goin ta take a recess here. We will convene at one-fifteen." The Rosey Gray filled up quickly, but most folks had brought their lunch and just found them a spot in front of the courthouse to eat.

Deputy Hill took Billy back down to Courtroom C and locked the door. Sheriff Tom stood in the hallway talking with Red and Ginger Pasko until he saw Ginger's eyes jerk and stare beyond his shoulder. He turned around and quickly shouted, "Where ya all think ya goin?" Cinder and Katey stopped. Cinder's eyes stilled and just stared at Sheriff Tom. Katey replied, "Theys say Billy be down there in a room. We thinkin maybe theys let us see him. Maybe we be allows ta sits wit him."

Sheriff Tom shouted, "Ya all git out of here. Ya hear me? Git on outside."

Cinder stood still. She gave a quick glance to the red-haired woman standing behind the sheriff. She saw her red eyes and dropped her own. Sheriff Tom shouted again, "Go on, now. Git out of here."

Cinder stood still.

Ginger Pasko reached for Sheriff Tom's arm, tugged at it until he turned around, then she just looked at him. He turned back to Cinder, looked at her, and said, "All right. Down there. Last door. Ya tell Deputy Hill that Sheriff Tom says it's all right." As Cinder passed, she glanced at Ginger Pasko again and their eyes met.

Deputy Hill opened the door when he heard the tapping knock, then let Cinder and Katey in after he looked up the hall and got Sheriff Tom's signal.

Billy jumped up from his chair and ran to his mother, then they sat in the room's noon shadow; the two figures became one shaded sketch. Cinder has Billy in her arms. She has brought him so close that he is her. Billy is snifflin, quiverin, as he says, "Ah wants ta goes home. Mama, they says Ah can't." Katey wiped the tears from her eyes and Deputy Hill looked away.

Cinder whispers, "Mama's here, Mama's here, baby."

Billy pleads again, "Mama, Ah wants ta go home. Ah don't wants ta be in that jail no more."

Cinder sighs as Billy cries and tries to talk through his tearful gasps. "Ah wants ta go home. Ah won't go ta that pond agin, Mama."

Cinder closes her eyes, but the dark does not come, just a faint speck of the color green, then the high green grass of green years ago, and Billy can play again, blue is in the sky, Mister Pete singin that old goin-home song, folks let her and her baby be. She kisses Billy, and the breath that carries his words and cries wisps across her lips. "They say Ah go wit ya? They say that? Ah don't wants ta be in a trial." Cinder is silent, but the dark comes, white face come into the night. Mister Pete's dead, been dead, ain't no sky, ain't no blues, greens die too.

Banes folks watched clocks tick away. The noon hour finally filled with minutes and moments. The courtroom swelled with chatter until Judge Harper called for order.

Billy jumped and looked around when he heard Gumpy's name being called. He heard Gumpy tellin the shoutin man, "He showed me his knife, its have blood on it. He say he stuck her in the titty. He say that too."

Ely Hampton kept pecking at Gumpy: "Where did Billy Lee keep his knife?"

Billy put his head back down and stared at the shades of the table before him. He can hear Gumpy calling, but it is in a different time. "Hey, Billy, can ya's come out? Hey, Billy, ya wants ta go down ta the Catfish wit me?" He can hear the sound of Gumpy's voice, but it is only the sound of his words. Gumpy is telling Ely Hampton, "It's be in his pocket. Cept if he wants ta cuts sumpin. If he gits mad at ya, he chase ya wit it. But he can't catch me. He can't runs like me."

Ely Hampton told Judge Harper, "The State rests its case, Your Honor."

Murmurs sizzled, necks twisted and turned, folks edged far up in their seats. Reverend Sims can see Billy as he jerks away from the sudden outstretched hand with the Bible in it. Then he sees him slowly touch the Bible with the coaxing and whispering of Matthew Brady.

Ginger Pasko shakes her head before turning away.

Cinder's heart pounds a thunderous sound.

Wilbur Braxton nears Billy on the witness stand and whispers something to him. Billy nods his head yes, but does not look up. "Tell the people what your name is, Billy," Wilbur Braxton says.

Billy remains silent.

Wilbur Braxton is patient, he repeats, "Billy, tell the people what your name is."

Billy's lips move, but no sound comes from his mouth.

"Are you afraid, Billy?"

Billy shakes his head no, squirms in the big chair, then nods his head yes.

"Come on, son, I told you there was nothing to be afraid of. Tell the people your name. You can do that."

"Billy Lee my name."

"Now, Billy, tell the people how old you are."

"Ah ten."

"Now, Billy, tell the people why you are here today."

"Ah don't knows. They says it's a trial."

"What's a trial, Billy? Tell the people what a trial is."

"Ah don't know."

"Billy, what happen to you at the pond? What happen, son?"

Billy is silent.

Red Pasko waits for an answer.

"What happen, Billy?"

"Them girls come. They beats me up. Theys bigger."

"Why did they beat you up?"

"Ah don'ts know. Me and Gumpy be in the pond. Theys come and git us."

"Did you try and run from the girls, Billy?"

"Ah runs, but theys catch me. That girl, she bigger than me. She gits me down."

"Billy, what happen when they let you up? Did you try and run again?"

"Ah gits up. She comes and gits me agins."

"Did she hit you again?"

"Ah stuck her. Ah make her leave me be."

"Billy, what happen to her?"

"Ah don't know. They says she deads."

"Billy, did you want to hurt her? Did you want to make her die?"

"Ah ain't makes her deads. She comes gits me agins. Ah stuck her. Ah makes her leave me be."

Red Pasko clenches his teeth.

Ely Hampton does not wait for Wilbur Braxton to take his seat before he is up shouting, "Billy Lee. Billy Lee, ya ever see this knife before?"

Billy puts his head down.

Ely Hampton holds the knife up and shouts, "Billy Lee. Look up here. This your knife, boy?"

Billy looks up, nods his head yes, and looks back down.

"Ya say ya stuck her with this knife? How many times you stick her?"

Billy is silent.

"How many times ya stick her, Billy Lee Turner? Ya stuck her pretty hard, didn't ya? Just wasn't a poke, was it? Ya lashed out at her. Ya slashed her arm first, so ya could plunge that knife up in her. Get it in there deep, didn't ya, boy?"

Billy utters, "She beats me up."

Ely Hampton walks away, goes back to his prosecuting table, then comes back to Billy carrying a bag in his hands. He reaches into the bag and pulls out Lori's blood-stained shirt.

Ginger Pasko's gasp cannot muffle her scream.

Ely Hampton holds Lori's shirt up in one hand and Billy's knife in the other and shouts, "Look up here, Billy Lee, look up here."

Slowly Billy looks up.

"This is your knife, Billy Lee, isn't it? This is the shirt Lori had on when ya plunged your knife into her. Isn't it? Answer me, Billy Lee Turner."

Big Jake puts his head down.

Katey utters a desperate whisper, "He ain't means it, Lord."

Billy sees the blood-stained shirt.

November's first day's sun was going down. Its soft yellow rays gently lay across the broken Patch Road. Cinder walked slowly. When she would stop and just stand and quiver, Big

Jake was near. Gently he would reach for her, bring her to
him so she could lean some of the way.

Katey followed; she was tired of the road and where it went
and where it came from. Reverend Sims walked by her side,
clutching his slavin Bible, but grasping for the faith he left
behind.

Cinder's screams still filled the courthouse; the echoes
wouldn't die. Ginger Pasko had heard the cries, but she did
not turn around to see, she knew who the woman would be.

Wilbur Braxton was still telling hisself that he had done
his best. He had told the jury, "I stand before you respectfully and humbly. Respectfully as you are men, humbly as I
am merely a man. We share a heavy burden today; we have
that child's life in our hands. My God, that child is no killer."

He had paced back and forth before the twelve faces, he
had tried to tell them, "What happened at that pond was a
tragedy. Children in fear and anger and a knife at hand. A
tragedy in our days. Storms, high waters, winds in the night
that blow down homes and shatter lives. We know our trage-
dies." Ginger Pasko had heard him say, "There is an empty
supper seat, Lori's seat; a cup of joy is bare and dry. But
there is a mightier force than man that lowers the high waters
of the storm, brings flowers to bear where there was only
scorn." Twelve silent faces heard him whisper his final plea:
"Please don't kill Billy too."

A silent moment had lingered over the court, perhaps too
long. Judge Harper cleared his throat and sent his jury away
to find its verdict. Banes folks went to waiting, but not too
long. Cinder had sat with Reverend Sims; he had told her,
"God cans show blind mens to see. He'll show em the rights
things ta do. Ya just gots ta believes."

Word of the jury's return spread through the streets and minds before time could gather its composure and pace itself with dignity. Quickly the courtroom filled, then stilled itself as the jury entered. Now only the sound of Matthew Brady's footsteps can be heard as he carries the verdict to Judge Harper. Patiently, the silence in the courtroom waited for Judge Harper to speak, then it ran into the corner and stood with Reverend Sims' God; and put its head down too.

Celebrants' shouts and chatter filled the courtroom until Cinder's screams trampled every sound.

12

Mississippi nights cooled, were sometimes chilling, coon dogs howl, and long roads stretch far into the night. Billy can see out the window from where he sits bouncing in the back of the State Prison van. The heavy leg irons and wrist shackles keep dragging on his thoughts, his thin bony body sways with the veers of the van, he sees the night sky following behind the dusty window.

Hattiesburg Prison's in Parks County, just on the other side of Greene County. It was built in the late eighteen hundreds and mostly holds Mississippi's criminals that are mentally insane and Mississippi's criminals that are waiting their executions. Death row sits at the far northern end of the prison yard, a separate building with its own fence around it. It was simply known as the Death House, its cellblock was numbered nine. At the tail end of the cellblock and behind the big heavy steel door is a corridor with white walls that look gray in the dim light. Twenty-five steps away, another door opens into an old storage area that has been converted into the death chamber's holding cell. The condemned were held there while final preparations were being attended to.

The electric chair itself sits back near the north wall of red bricks. It's bolted down into the cement floor, black rubber matting covers the floor around it. It is a big wooden chair, dark wood, wood without color to one's eyes, with worn rawhide straps hanging from its arms and legs. At the top of its high straight back, hanging loosely, is the gray metal headpiece. Far off to the side of the chair, a corner of the room has been made into a closet-size area containing the chair's electric generator, and enough space for the executioner to do his work. Eight feet in front of the chair, a small handrail goes across the room; behind the handrail are four rows of seats, four seats to a row, for spectators and official witnesses.

Condemned men were brought into the room, led by Warden Casey Herman, a short man of sixty-four years of age. A chaplain, if requested by the condemned, would follow the man's final steps and chant prayers to his awaiting God. Some men walked strong, would not bow to death. Others staggered, leaned on guards, crouched and cringed away from their doom. All would be seated, strapped, then the ceremony would begin. Last words would be said, last words would be heard.

Billy watches the night follow the window until the van slows and stops, then he tries to listen and tries to hear the voices in the night.

"Whatcha got for us tonight, Barney?" a voice outside the van shouted.

"Gots that little Banes nigger." The shout is closer and comes from up front of the van.

"Yeah, we expectin him. Take him on over. Ed got the duty tonight." The shout fades into the night. Billy listens to the slow clanking sound as the van moves forward. Lights come into the dark, Billy can see them out the window, see them hanging, and flickering. The van stops, then the lights come into Billy's face.

"Come on out of there, boy. Get out here, now."

Billy shifts and drags his chain to the opened van door.

"Come on, boy, ya get on out here, now."

The lights make Billy squint, the leg irons cause him to stumble and nearly fall to the ground.

"Git up, boy. Ain't nobody carryin ya around here."

Ed Welte is the night-watch sergeant, a tall heavy man with a quick way about him. He watches Billy gather his balance, calls to the driver, "See ya next trip. Tell old Bentley Ah says hello," then looks down at Billy and shouts, "Follow me, boy. Ya just keep ya eyes on my back and follow me."

Ed Welte turns on his heels and walks towards the heavy door, yells through a slit in its center, "Open up."

Billy sees the big door open and the wall of bars. He is used to the big men's ways now, he has learned to move to his keepers' calls, learned to listen while footsteps leave, listen until he can't hear them at all, before he moves, climbs up to find out if he can see through a window.

"What the hell is this? Whatcha got there, Ed?" a voice behind the wall of bars rings out.

"This is that Banes nigger, ya know, the one that knifed that girl to death. Just got him in," Ed Welte yells to the guard behind the gate.

A center door in the wall of bars comes open, Billy knows

it is for him, he drags his legs irons and wobbles his body through.

"Come here, boy, get over here, stand still." Ed Welte points to where he wants Billy to stand.

Billy lowers his head and jumps a little when the big man goes behind him and kneels to unlock his leg irons, then comes around to his front and takes his wrist irons off.

"Step here, now, ya follow me." Ed Welte moves and Billy follows him through another door, and then another.

"Stand right here. Don't ya move," the guard shouts and opens a closet.

"Here, boy, ya get one blanket. Ya piss on it, ya sleep on it. Here, come get it. Now, follow me." Ed Welte leads Billy down a long dark hall to a door of bars.

"Open up here, got us a new one."

The door of bars slides open. Except for a dim light, the walkway ahead is dark, cells along each side. Snores and heavy breathing can be heard, but the air is tight and hard to breathe.

Ed Welte stops up short, takes his key, and opens the cell he has turned to.

"Get on in there, boy, and Ah don't want ta hear no noise out of ya. Ya do whatcha told when ya told ta do it, for the time ya here. Ya ain't gonna have no trouble outta me, but ya start actin up, ya gonna wish ya hadn't. Now, get on in there."

"Boss man Welte, what's ya got over there? Who that? They gonna burn that boy? Who that?"

"Shut up, Sack Man," Ed Welte shouts into the dark cell across from Billy's.

"Hey, Sack Man, we git us some new meat? Whatcha got up there? Meat wagon come in? What we git?" comes a voice from further up in the darkness.

"Shut up, god damn it," Ed Welte shouts and locks Billy in his cell, then turns and leaves.

Shouts come from the dark again.

"Hey, Sack Man, we git somethin new up there? Where they put him, they put him in Tinker's cell?"

Billy puts his blanket on the bottom of the cot, then tries to look around his dark cell. He looks up on the wall, there is no window.

"Hey. Hey, boy. Hey," comes a whisper across the walkway.

Billy moves to the bars and peeps out through them, his eyes search the darkness in the cell across from his until he sees the face come out of it. It's a big face as dark as the dark, the face of Sack Man, Raymond "Sack Man" Tate. He is fifty-three and won't get any older. The State of Mississippi found him guilty of killin a man with a hatchet, then robbing his house. Sack Man is a big man with only one arm, said he got his other arm cut off fightin Germans in the big war, said he lived up north in Chicago Town and would have stayed if things hadn't got so bad, said he had to kill that man before he got his gun.

Sack Man whispers to Billy, "Boy, what's they got ya in here for? How old ya be? Ya ain't buts a child. What's they doin? What ya do, huh?"

Billy looks up into the dark and its face, then whispers, "Ah gonna be electrics. They say they do that ta me. They say that makes me dead."

"What ya do, boy?"

"Ah stuck a girl. She tries and beats me up. Gits me down again."

"Did ya kill her, is she dead?"

"They say she killed. They say she deads."

"Boy, how old ya? How old ya be, son?"

"Ah ten, but Ah be leven in Febueries."

A sneering piercing whisper comes from far in the dark.

"Hey, Sack Man. Hey, Sack Man, what we got up there? Sounds like we got us a little pussy, we got us a pussy up there?" The far whisper comes from Dil Martin, thirty-two, with black curly hair, blue eyes, and a baby's face. He shot two men to death in a bar in Jackson, then shot one of Jackson's policemen in the leg.

In the cell next to Dil Martin is Gilbert Knox, he's awake but just setting in the dark like he always does. Gilbert Knox is twenty-seven, lived outside Biloxi on a small farm with his mama, daddy, and two sisters until he killed all four of them with a shotgun. You ask him about it, he just laughs and says, "They got on my nerves." He is next to die.

Sack Man moves back into the dark of his cell, but Dil Martin's whispers still come. "Sack Man, hey, Sack Man. We gots us a little boy-girl up there, huh?"

"Shut up, crazy man, shut up," Sack Man yells.

"Hee . . . hee . . . hee . . . hee . . ." Dil Martin's taunting laugh wiggles through the dark cellblock.

Billy sits on his cot with his blanket over his shoulder, he is cold now and begins to shiver.

"Hey, boy. Hey, boy, you up there, hey, you. This is Dil Martin down here. Dil Martin. You hear of me, boy? You ever hear of me, huh? Huh? You hear of me, answer me, boy," Dil Martin calls again.

Billy crawls on his cot and pulls the blanket over his head, he can see more in his nights than his long days. In his days, he can only see cracks in hard cement floors, cracks in dark walls, watch the shadows lift and move slowly across the cell. In his days, he may only get a glimpse of Cinder, a glimpse of the Catfish, the red Patch Road, Gumpy waitin on the path, but the nights, Cinder brings the Catfish Creek, Patch ways, and Gumpy to stay, until the morning comes, then they run away.

Mississippi's sun comes up, dark-gray walls and thick black bars lighten but do not become bright. Food comes to cellblock nine, but the shouts and grunts come first. All five condemned souls, Sack Man, Dil Martin, Gilbert Knox, Preacher Man Sam, and Jimmy Johnson, know of the sixth, Billy Lee Turner.

Day Guard Russell Vent comes to see what the night has brung. Billy sits on his cot and looks up at the guard looking in at him and waits for his barking words, but instead hears the shouts of "Boss man Vent, how bout bringin that boy down here, let him spend some time with Dil here, whatcha say, boss man Vent?"

"Shut up, Martin," the guard yells over his shoulder, then walks away.

"Hey, Billy boy," Sack Man calls.

"Huh," Billy answers and goes to his bars.

"You listen to old Sack Man here, don't ya pay that old crazy fool down there no mind, you hear me? He ain't nothin but a crazy fool," Sack Man whispers across the walkway.

Billy begins to talk, ask questions of Sack Man, then slowed his words and stared at Sack Man's missing arm until Sack Man tells him of the big war and the Germans. Then the talk becomes Chicago, the Catfish, and, "My mama, she comes gits me." Time left them alone.

Dil Martin calls out for Preacher Man Sam, "Hey, Preacher Man, Preacher Man, how many days ya got? How many ya got left now? Ya countin right? How many days ya got fore they burn ya to hell? Hee ... hee ... hee ... Tell me, Preacher Man. Ya gonna preach to that old devil? Ya gonna tell him he ought ta change his ways some? They gonna like ya down there. They gonna just think you the best thing that ever come down there."

Preacher Man Sam was a pickin man from down in Dillard County, big flabby yellow-skinned man with little beady eyes that look blodshot all the time. State of Mississippi knew he killed his wife and children and tried to hang them up on big crosses he made for them. He told the State they had the devil in them. Preacher Man Sam comes to his cell bars and shouts, "Lord's day a comin, Lord's day a comin, gonna be thunder and lightnin likes ya ain't never seen."

"Shut the fuck up. Shut up, you crazy-ass nigger," Jimmy Johnson shouts from his cell. He is a tall slender man of thirty-five with dark brown but shiny skin. He came back to Jackson from New York City with some of them big-city ways. Debbie Ross, a twenty-four-year-old Jackson white woman, said Jimmy Johnson raped her. Jimmy Johnson said she couldn't stay away from him.

The night and days began to creep by. The days were, "Hey, Sack Man, ya see them big buildins up there in Chicago? Ya see a picture show? Ah seen em big buildins in my mama's picture books. They's big, huh?"

The nights had a different way, if the lights came on, the silence came. It would be someone's time. The guards and the warden would follow the sound of the big door being opened.

The lights come on.

Billy wakes and sits on his cot. The sound of footsteps near, and then he watches men walk by. He hears them stop and a cell door clank open, then a big voice saying, "Gilbert Knox, it's time. Are you ready?" Shuffling sounds come, and muffled words, then the sound of the cell door closing and the footsteps going away. The lights go back off and the night goes on.

A day or so later, Wilson Wagner came, he lived right down

the road from the prison, in the little town of Troyville, he is a preacher and the prison chaplain. Wilson Wagner is a small thin man with slow ways and calm eyes, he comes to see Billy on his weekly rounds. Guard Russell Vent comes with him.

Billy hears the locked door opened and the footsteps coming and looks up from his cot.

"Billy, how ya doin, son?" Wilson Wagner asks.

Billy is silent and just stares.

"Russell, why don't ya open up and let me sit awhile with this boy."

Billy watches his cell door being opened and squirms back on his cot, but keeps his eyes on the man who is nearing him.

Wilson Wagner sits gently down on Billy's cot and looks at him a moment before saying, "Billy, I'm Reverend Wilson Wagner. I'm the chaplain here at the prison. Most of the men call me Wil. I've come to see how you're doing."

Billy puts his head down and is only silent.

Wilson Wagner smiles a little, reaches over and puts his hand on Billy's shoulder, and says, "I heard ya were here, and I brought ya something I think ya just might like. Ya like these?"

The Chaplain reaches into his pocket and brings out two candy bars. Billy sees his hand move, hears the crackling of the candy wrap, and looks into the Chaplain's hand, then looks up at his face.

"Go on, son, take them, they're yours," Wilson Wagner whispers.

Billy reaches for the candy bars and then sets peeling off one of the wrappers.

"How old are ya, son?" Wilson Wagner asks what he already knows.

"Ah ten. Ah be leven in Febueries."

"Sack Man over there takin care of ya?" Wilson Wagner says loud enough for Sack Man to hear.

"Sack Man my friend. Him and me friends. He be in Chicago. He be in a big war wit Germans," Billy says with quick words and big eyes.

Wilson Wagner smiles as Billy goes on about Sack Man, then ask, "Billy, do you know about Jesus? Did ya go ta Sunday school?"

Billy is still thinking about Sack Man, but his thoughts slow as he sees the Patch church in his mind and he can hear Reverend Sims hollerin, and answers, "Ah goes sometime. Katey make me go."

"Is Katey ya mama?"

"My mama Cinder. Katey be my aunt, she be goin down the Sunday church all the times. She takes me sometime."

"Did ya hear them talkin about Jesus Christ? Did they tell ya about Him?" Wilson Wagner leans closer to Billy, whispers about Jesus, waits for Billy to speak of Him.

"He be born in a stable, He be born there wit animals all round and angels some too."

"Can ya read, Billy? Can ya read the Bible?"

"Ah can read some words, not them big kind. My mama, she show me how to read some words in her picture books."

Wilson Wagner tells Billy some stories, tries to explain what his faith is to him. "Faith, Billy, is, is believin. Thinkin real hard about somethin ya can't see but want to, and thinkin real hard about it, waitin for it to come, no matter what anyone says. Ya still think hard about somethin ya want and wait for it to come. It's like when ya go fishin, ya can't see the fish deep in the water, but ya have faith that they are there, and pretty soon ya get one."

Wilson Wagner is silent for a moment and takes a deep sigh, then says, "Billy, ya got to keep ya faith, son, ya got to pray for Jesus to save ya. He can do it."

Billy's days go slow, start with first light, food, and Sack Man. Late eve would come, and sometimes an early silence. Sack Man told Billy, "It's Jimmy's time." In the night the lights came on, the footsteps came, Billy watched them pass and heard Wilson Wagner talkin about his Jesus.

Mississippi's December came and its eighteenth day with its first light, its food, and its morning grunts, moans, and shouts. But Sack Man was quiet.

"Hey, Sack Man. Sack Man, what ya doin?" Billy calls across the walkway, where he sees Sack Man still sittin on his cot.

Sack Man doesn't answer, turns away, and looks at the wall.

Dil Martin shouts over Billy's calls, "Hey, Sack Man, Ah bet they gonna give it to ya real slow, let ya simmer . . . Hee . . . hee . . . hee . . . Yes sir, Ah bet they gonna let ya simmer just like a old fat hog on a spit."

Preacher Man Sam starts, "Lord a comin, He's just a comin. Gonna get all ya sinners. Bury ya in His hell. He's a comin. . . ."

Dil Martin shouts back at the Preacher Man, "Shut up, ya old crazy asshole, ya next. Hee . . . hee . . . hee . . . ya next, ya fat asshole. When they get ya fat ass in there, they gonna keep that hot juice on till all that fat melt off. Hee . . . hee."

"Lord's a comin. Lord's just a comin . . . ," Preacher Man keeps on preachin.

Billy shouts over the Preacher Man's hollerin, "Sack Man, Sack Man, they's electrics ya? It be ya time, huh? Theys come and gits ya tonight, Sack Man?"

The day passes slowly and silently for Billy, then nears its end.

"Billy boy, ya just remember them words Wil be teachin ya, and ya remember old Sack Man. Um readies for my time, been ready, done seen my days. Ain't sorry for too many things. Sorry abouts that mans Ah had ta do what Ah did, but Ah sorrier for what they doin ta ya. Ifs Ah gits up there and sees Jesus, Um gonna tells Him ta takes care of ya." Sack Man spoke slowly as he leaned on his cell bars and watched the day's light fade in the high window over the cellblock wall.

Nighttime and the dark comes. Billy sits quietly on his cot, from time to time he gets up and presses his face against his bars and stares across the walkway into Sack Man's cell. Except for Dil Martin's shouts that come and last until he laughs, the night is quiet. Billy waits with Sack Man.

The lights come on, the cellblock door clanks open, the footsteps come. Billy sits on his cot and watches as the guard men and the warden man gather in front of Sack Man's cell, he hears Wilson Wagner's voice, but cannot see him. Another voice speaks, "Well, Sack Man, I'm sorry, but it's time."

Sack Man stands in his cell, looks around as his door is being opened, then steps slowly out into the walkway and whispers somethin to Warden Herman. Warden Herman nods his head yes, then says, "Hurry it up."

Sack Man comes to Billy's cell and peers through the bars, then he speaks in a low soft voice, "Billy boy . . ."

Billy jumps from his cot and runs up to the bars with tears in his eyes.

"Billy boy, Sack Man's goin now. Ya do what Reverend Wil say. Ya keeps that faith he be tellin ya about." Sack Man speaks and reaches his hand in between Billy's bars and puts it on Billy's cheek. Then it's time. He turns and takes his steps.

Billy twists his head as far as he can to watch Sack Man leave him, then yells before he knows he is yelling, "Sack Man. Sack Man."

The lights go back out and even Dil Martin is still in the silence.

The new year that time brought, nineteen hundred and thirty-eight, didn't much change things back in Banes. Town folks did the same thing they did the year before, Dillion Street still had its Saturday nights, Sheriff Tom was still bustin heads, Doctor Henry P. Grey was still sewing them up. Fred Sneed was still sittin across from the Rosey Gray, and Marcus Warden sold some more coffins.

January crept by and February took its place. It was February's third Saturday, Harvey Jakes sits in his office alone, waiting for Helen Marks to stop by, he'd asked her to come, said he wanted to ask her something. He hears her heels coming through the outer office and looks up from his desk as she comes in wearing the short skirt he likes to see her in. Her long blond hair was down and curling over her shoulders. Her step was quick until she reached his desk, then she slowed, looked down, and smiled. Harvey Jakes leaned back in his chair and says, "Glad you could stop by, this will only take a minute. I got some good news."

"I'm getting excited, you've been teasing since Thursday about this good news," Helen Marks says, smiling and easing closer to Harvey Jakes' desk.

"You've been doing a good job, Helen, and, ah . . . well, I've been thinking . . ." Harvey Jakes' words fade.

Helen Marks was becoming very impatient with Harvey

Jakes, she puts her hands on her hips and looks him in the eye until he says what she wants to hear.

"Well, the good news is that I have permission from the State to witness the execution. It will be a great chance for a first-person story," Harvey Jakes says and keeps his eyes on Helen Marks for her reaction.

"You what?"

"I got permission to cover the execution."

"That's great, Mister Jakes. If ya want to watch that little nigger die," Helen Marks says with some disappointment in her voice.

"Well, what I really was thinking, Helen, was maybe you'd like to ride up with me. It's a nice ride. Of course, we'd have to stay over, I mean, you would have your own room. I thought you might like to ride up." Harvey Jakes looks into Helen Marks' eyes for her answer.

Helen Marks is silent for a moment, her eyes smile, then she says, "I'd like to ride up with you, it sounds exciting. When is it?"

"Next Friday night."

Ginger Pasko is fixing evening supper, Red Pasko is out on the porch. Time changed him when it took his daughter away, he no longer tries to hide his drinking. He sits out on the porch with his whiskey glass, looking over the fields. The whiskey helps clear his mind of the colors of the field, the chill in the air, now he can peacefully think about next Friday. It's the day he's been waiting for.

Most Patch folks and Patch ways took well with Mississippi's nineteen hundred and thirty-eight year. It brought no less than the others. The old Patch Road still ran red and eventually to LeRoy's.

Big Jake sat at his table with his Saturday whiskey, drinkin and payin no mind to Shorty and LeRoy's talk until Lucy Mae came down.

"Ya want a little sip?" LeRoy asks Lucy Mae as she sits at the counter. She nods her head yes. LeRoy turns to Shorty, who has become his do-everything boy for a drink, and yells, "Shorty, git Lucy Mae somethin here."

Lucy Mae takes her drink slow as LeRoy and Shorty go on with their talk.

Big Jake busts into LeRoy and Shorty's talk, sayin, "Ya all need to stay off that woman. She gots trouble nobody knows."

LeRoy throws his words over to Big Jake. "What Ah can't see is why she still got her ass all up ta folks."

Lucy Mae pokes her cheeks out and rolls her eyes before sayin, "Ah knows if it be me, and theys be bout ta kills my childs, Ah be over cross the road all down on my knees. She just a bitch, still actin like she made outta gold just cause her skin that color. Shit, if it ain't been for her and them ways she got, my baby Gumpy be home, ain't be up in no camp prison, he be home."

"How ya see it that way?" Big Jake's words come quick.

"Shit, she ain't taught that boy right. She ain't taught Billy Lee a damn thing, cept he somethin special just cause he be hers. That boy just like her, and that daddy of his too. Ah knew sooner or later he gonna get Gumpy in trouble," Lucy Mae shouts back to Big Jake and rolls her eyes back to her drink.

"Ah tell ya what Ah thinkin," Shorty blurts out, looks around quickly to see if anyone is payin him mind, then he lets his mouth loose, "Ah tells ya, things ain't been the same, ain't never gonna be the same agins since that boy kills that girl. Ah ain't never takin myself up there agins, even them good white folks done change their ways. Ah tells ya whats

Ah know." Shorty nods his head at his own last words, then tilted his glass up to his mouth.

"When they goin ta kill that boy? What it be, end of the month?" LeRoy asks.

Reverend Sims had walked the Patch paths, he had gone and seen Cinder every day. Sometimes she'd come out and sit, but she wouldn't talk. He'd just sit too. Sometimes she'd talk, just a few words, then her silence would say the rest. Next Thursday he will go with her to see Billy for her last time, Katey has asked him to.

Cinder's time could no longer be measured by clocks and calendars, suns coming up, moons showing hafe their faces, springtimes coming. Cinder's time is measured now by only her heartbeats, pounding beneath her breast, and one thought that would not stop ripping at her mind, pinching at her soul. Time no longer gave her days and nights, only its ghost of a moment to come. Reverend Sims had spoke of his God, said He could change Cinder's world around, bring Billy home one day. Cinder said He should have never taken him away. Reverend Sims said, He'll bring him back one day. Cinder said, When, after the fires turn red, after they burn him dead, after they take the life from him? But I'll still love him. They can take him from me, but they can't take me from him.

Wilson Wagner had brought Billy some picture books and a Bible to read, along with some pencils, crayons, and paper to write and draw on too. Each day now, he'd come and sit with Billy, then prayed with and for him. He'd also written the Governor, got no reply, but had faith and told Billy of it.

Thursday, Guard Russell Vent comes to get Billy, Wilson Wagner is with him. Guard Russell Vent opens Billy's cell and says, "Come on, boy. Your mama's here."

Billy's eyes burst wide open and he jumps up and down. Guard Russell Vent is going to put the wrist irons on him until Wilson Wagner says, "For God's sake, man."

Cinder, Katey, Reverend Sims, and Wilbur Braxton wait in the special visitors' room, the one reserved for lawyers and clients and the one last family visit.

Cinder has not been able to see Billy since the trial, she sits staring at the door he'll come through. The guard captain had told them, "Four hours, and that's that. Ya got from twelve to four."

Now the door pops open and Guard Russell Vent peeks his head in, looks around, opens the door wider, and Billy comes in with Wilson Wagner behind him. Cinder jumps from her seat and runs to Billy, falls to her knees and wraps her arms around him, and just holds him.

"Mama ... Mama ... Mama ..." Billy cries.

Cinder's sighs fill the room, Guard Russell Vent looks around and takes a seat in the corner. Katey thanks her God.

Cinder leans back from Billy and looks into his eyes, then slowly takes her hand and gently wipes the tears away from his cheeks and just stares at him.

"Mama, ya comin ta git me? Theys say Ah go home?"

Cinder can't answer, but pulls him back into her arms.

Wilson Wagner looks away, then introduces hisself to Wilbur Braxton and Reverend Sims. "I'm Reverend Wilson Wagner, I'm the prison chaplain. I want ya to know I despise this. I've written the Governor and I still have faith, but in the event it is God's will, I promise I will be with Billy every minute."

Wilbur Braxton expresses his frustration, then lowers his head. Reverend Sims says he knows God too, and that he'd also talked to Him and knew things would be of His will.

Then the men sit at the table while Cinder and Katey keep Billy in their arms.

Cinder's eyes become strong for Billy, but Katey's eyes rain tears. When she could, Katey tries to get both Cinder and Billy into her arms. Katey's prayers could not remain silent, "Oh good Jesus, good Jesus, please be wit these childrens. Be wit em, Jesus." Her prayers become sighs and pants.

Cinder looks at Billy, looks him up and down, he looks pathetic in a man's shirt that hangs like a nightgown on him and trousers that look like they been cut off at the knees but still hung past his ankles. Yet his face had filled and it looked like he'd picked up a couple pounds.

"You getting big," she whispers, then says, "I miss you, baby. Mama thinks of you all the time. I love you, Billy Lee, nothing gonna change that."

She takes Billy to the table and sits beside him.

Wilbur Braxton sighs and looks at Billy's eyes, watches them bounce from face to face at the table, then he asks him how he is doing.

"Ah reads and draws pictures like in the picture books. Ah draw big buildins like theys has in Chicago. Sack Man, he tells me about picture shows he be seein, he say theys got lots of em in Chicago." Billy's words come quick. Wilson Wagner glances away from the table when he hears the words were of Sack Man. He sees the straps around Sack Man's stump arm, then saw it almost slide out when he was jolted by the first shock.

"Theys come gits Sack Man. Theys electrics him."

Cinder's eyes flash at Guard Russell Vent, then to the dark wood of the table before she brings them back to Billy.

Wilson Wagner tells Cinder what a good reader Billy's be-

come and what a good boy he is, then asks Billy to tell his
mother what he's learned about Jesus.

Billy blushes and looks down at the floor.

"Come, Billy, tell your mama what you learned, and what
you can say," Wilson Wagner eases Billy on.

"Ah knows about He forgives ya. He die too, He dies on
the cross for everybodies, and he be there waitin for ya when
ya dies," Billy says and looks at Cinder. She smiles.

Wilson Wagner asks, "What can ya almost say now, Billy?
What have ya been learning to say? I bet your mama and
Aunt Katey would like to hear you say it."

Billy blushes again and looks away until Katey says,
"What ya done learned, child? What ya done learned to
say?"

Cinder keeps her eyes on Billy as he slowly looks at her
and says, "Ah can'ts say it all."

Wilson Wagner says, "Just say the first part, then, Billy, ya
know that."

Billy's eyes close for a moment, then open as he blurts out,
"The Lords be my shepherd, Ah shalls not wants. . . . He's
makin . . . uh . . . me lays down in green pastures. . . . He
stores my soul. . . . He . . . uh . . . uh . . . He . . ." Billy's
words fade.

"God bless ya, child," Katey gasps.

Talk takes its time, Cinder keeps her eyes from the clock,
but when it is quiet, she hears its ticking.

Wilbur Braxton watches the clock.

Reverend Sims prays silently.

Guard Russell Vent begins to stir in his chair, then nods
when he catches Wilson Wagner's eye. Wilson Wagner taps
Reverend Sims on his shoulder and whispers, "Would ya like
to lead us in a prayer?"

Cinder begins to quiver as she knows her time is coming to its end, both her arms go around Billy.

Reverend Sims stands and bows his head.

Wilbur Braxton, Wilson Wagner, and Katey remain seated but lower their faces, Guard Russell Vent looks out the window.

"Dear God, heavenly Father," Reverend Sims begins.

Cinder closes her eyes and just holds Billy.

"Look down from your heavens, Lord," the prayer is coming.

"Mama, Mama, can ya takes me?" Billy ask in Cinder's ear.

"See this mother and child, see em, Jesus."

"Mama, Ah wants ta go home. Ah wants ta go with ya," Billy pleads.

"Give em yer strength today, let em lean on ya, Jesus."

Cinder can't open her eyes, she just pulls Billy closer.

"Jesus forgives this boy's sins. Forgive him, Jesus."

"Ah don'ts wants ta be electrics, Mama, Ah scared."

"Lord have mercy. Have mercy. Have mercy on this child, give ya mercy ta this mother. Hear our prays in this time of need. Give em ya strength ta carry through this time. Lift their burdens of the soul. Lift their burdens of this here despair and fill their hearts, their souls with the mighty hope of God. The mighty hope of everlastin life in Jesus Christ, Savior of the world. Amen."

The prayer has ended.

Guard Russell Vent comes to his feet and nods to Wilson Wagner.

Wilbur Braxton stands, sighs, looks at Cinder holding Billy, and whispers, "It's time. We must go."

Cinder is silent, but Katey begins to cry loudly.

Guard Russell Vent begins to near.

Wilbur Braxton whispers again, "We have to go."

Reverend Sims moves forward and places his hand on Cinder's shoulder, then, in a moment, he whispers to her, "Ya gots ta leave him with God now. He'll takes care of him. Ain't no better caretaker than the Lord."

Cinder is silent, but begins to shake.

"Ah wants ta go homes. Take me wit ya, Mama. Ah won'ts stick nobodies agins. Ah won'ts," Billy whimpers and begins to cry.

"Time up. Time's up here," Guard Russell Vent says over Billy's cries.

"Miss Turner, we have to go now." Wilbur Braxton comes to Cinder's side.

Guard Russell Vent comes forward and grabs Billy's arm.

Cinder jerks Billy away from him and screams, "NO . . . NO . . . NO . . . NEVER." Her screams pierce through the walls, the doors, smash through windows, burst the outside air, "NO . . . NO . . . YA CAN'T HAVE HIM. NO."

The door flies open and more guards come in, then look at Guard Russell Vent. "Git him out of here," Guard Russell Vent shouts and grabs Billy's arm and pulls, while saying to Wilbur Braxton, "Ya got ta git her out of here, git this women out of here."

Wilbur Braxton and Reverend Sims take Cinder's arms in their hands and hold them gently, but firmly.

Wilson Wagner comes to Cinder's ear and whispers frantically, "I'll be with him, Miss Turner, I'll be with him. I'll stay with him, I promise ya, there's still hope, there's still hope, Miss Turner, the Governor can call, he can call, Miss Turner, he can call. . . ."

The guards wedge their hands in between Cinder and Billy, then rip him from her arms.

"NO, NO. BILLY, BILLY, BILLY, BILLY, NO," Cinder screams with empty arms.

Billy tries to look over his shoulder as he is yanked through the doorway, but he cannot see his mother, only hears her calling his name. He cries out to her, "Mama, gits me. Gits me, Mama."

Billy was still crying and shaking when he was taken to the prison barber, he had to be held still in the chair as the barber man made sure all his hair was gone and the electricity would have no distraction.

The February eve was starting, Thursday was fading.

Billy sits alone in his cell, food had come and now was gone. Preacher Man Sam had vanished nights ago, only Dil Martin was spared from the footsteps in the night. New faces set in the dark.

The cellblock door clanks open, footsteps come and stop at Billy's cell. Guard Ed Welte and Warden Casey Herman stand at Billy's cell bars, the warden speaks.

"How ya doin, Billy?"

Billy looks up, then looks back down.

Warden Casey Herman speaks slowly and softly.

"Billy Lee Turner, it's my regret, but duty here, to inform you that there has been no stay of your execution. Therefore, unless we receive word from the Governor, the State of Mississippi is prepared to go forth with the scheduled execution one minute after tomorrow's midnight. Ya be removed from your cell at precisely eleven P.M. and taken to the holding cell. You may and as I understand you will have in your presence Chaplain Wilson Wagner. You'll remain in your holding cell until eleven-fifty-five, at which time you'll be taken from your holding cell to the execution room. Chaplain Wagner will be able to accompany you. At the precise moment of one minute past twelve o'clock, the State of Mississippi will carry out its death warrant. I understand your burial arrangements have been taken care of by Attorney Wilbur Braxton of Banes County."

Warden Casey Herman sighs as he finishes his duty and looks down at Billy sitting and staring at the floor.

Warden Casey Herman has one more thing to say.

"Billy, son, I'm sorry."

Night comes quickly after the eve but not before Dil Martin shouts out of his dark, "Hey, boy, ya gonna burn tomorrow, ya want ta come down here and spend ya last night with Dil Martin? Give me a good old mouth job? Ah bet ya can really give one, can't ya? Hey, boy, ya hear Dil talkin ta ya? Hee . . . hee . . . hee . . ."

"Shut the fuck up, asshole. Let the boy be," Rufus Hays shouts, he is a new face that waits.

Billy climbs under his blanket and closes his eyes so he can see Cinder.

The last day of February fell, its first-light hour broke open the day. Except for a few dogs chasing cats and howling, Banes streets were empty and silent, but Sheriff Tom sits at his desk scribblin. He had spent the night at the jail, the two prisoners downstairs were not to be trusted. The sheriff scribbled and waited for the day to hurry along and bring Deputy Hill with it, so he could go home for a while. When the streets were a little lighter, Deputy Hill came in.

"Mornin, Sheriff. Get any sleep?"

The sheriff mumbles somethin and keeps scribbling, doesn't say nothing Deputy Hill can understand. Deputy Hill pours a cup of coffee and comes over to the sheriff's desk and says, "Well, Ah guess it's that boy's last day. Change your mind about goin up?"

The sheriff shakes his head no and glances at his watch, then says, "I'm gonna get outta here. Be back in two or three hours. Get them two somethin from the Rosey Gray, and watch em, they think they're slick."

Sheriff Tom leaves the office and heads home. Ely Hampton had asked him to ride up with him for the execution, but he told Ely Hampton no.

Deputy Hill sits behind the sheriff's desk with his cup of coffee, he looks down at the scribbled-up desk pad and wonders if the sheriff slept at all. Most of the time, the sheriff's scribblings was nothin more than zigs-and-zags pencil marks, or scratchy-written names, never words that made sense to him, unless it was the name of some fugitive. Deputy Hill didn't fully understand what the sheriff meant by the scribbling he left. The words were scratchy, but he could see they said, "better way of living or dying somewhere."

Doctor Henry P. Grey was woke, but not out of his bed yet, his wife was just awaking. When she opened her eyes, she noticed he was already wide awake and asked if he had slept well or at all. He'd been quiet in his thoughts the eve before and she'd asked if he was troubled about the execution. He had said yes. He'd said he never could get used to folks taking what he spent all his life keeping and caring for.

Banes' morning was getting brighter. Fred Sneed comes out to sit in its sun, Dexter Clayton and J. J. Gates weren't too far behind him. After their "Good mornin" and their shiftin their sittin stools around to get in or out of the sun, it wasn't too long after that they got to talkin.

It was quiet for a moment until J. J. Gates says, "Well, Ah still say hangin best. It been done back when it happened, rest of the niggers know right then, by this time a nigger forgets."

Fred Sneed looks J. J. Gates right in the eye and says, "Hangin's too good for em. Ought ta do what them boys down in Greene did when they caught that one crazy nigger down there, hog-gut him good, that's what they did. Hog-gut him good, then hung him up in their nigger nest over there for them other niggers ta see, that's the way it ought ta be done. Do it like that, a nigger can understand. A nigger ain't forget it that way."

Dexter Clayton yawns, spits a little tobacco juice, then says, "Well, gots one thing for sure, that nigger ain't goin ta be alive this time tomorrow."

Ely Hampton is over at Hanner's cuttin shop.

"What time ya leavin ta go up, Ely?" Mister Hanner asks as talk gets to the execution.

"Ah reckon about five will get us there in plenty time."

"Ya know, I still say folks got a right to see. Ought ta make it public again and have it right there where they did the crime. That way, niggers and anybody else got killin on their mind can see what they got comin, that's what I say," Mister Hanner says, and looks around the shop for approval from his other two waiting customers.

Ely Hampton says quickly, "Can't say I disagree, can't say I do, but that's the law now."

Jay Vasser, he's next to get his hair cut, asks, "What time they goin ta do the killin?"

"Twelve precisely. Warden Herman up there is a good man, runs things by the book. Good orderly man," says Ely Hampton.

Jay Vasser leans back in his chair and says, "Ah sure would like to see it myself."

Helen Marks is excited about her trip, she's told her family she will have her own hotel room and will help write the big story. She comes into the newspaper office early so her and Harvey Jakes can get a good start on the road, and get there in time to get good rooms and supper. She's been teasing Harvey Jakes about his professional manners he shows. "You're so proper all the time," she says as Harvey Jakes checks his last-minute details for the trip.

"Helen, I just want to make sure I have all the clips on the story so far, and have my credentials in order. I don't want any last-minute problems."

"Oh, Mister Jakes, you'll write the best story up there, I know you will," Helen Marks says with a smile on her face, then asks, "Mister Jakes, you ever see somebody die before? What's it like?"

Harvey Jakes is silent for a moment and continues to pick at the papers on his desk, then sighs and says, "No, I've seen a lot of dead folks, but I can't say I've seen somebody die."

Helen Marks lowers her eyes, then looks up without her smile and asks, "Mister Jakes, I wonder what it's like. I mean, I wonder what it's really like to be electrocuted."

At the far end of Dillion Street, and off to its side, Pete Grayson sits quietly at his breakfast table with his wife and daughter, Kelly. He has talked less than usual and keeps looking away from the table to the window. His wife, Holly, asks, "Ya got that rheumatism up again? I told ya to be more careful with this weather."

Pete Grayson remains quiet, but turns back to the table.

His daughter, Kelly, stops eating and stares at her father with that piercing look she can get and asks, "Daddy, what's wrong with you?"

"Ah wish you two'd stop frettin bout nothin," Pete Grayson says quickly, but the thoughts in his mind do not move. He keeps seeing long-ago hot nights down by the Catfish bridge, sees Alma sneaking through the tall grass and coming to him. Alma had cried when she told him of the child she was carrying, his child. Now it is his other daughter, Cinder, he thinks of without having any words to put on his feeling. He has forbidden such words to enter his mind, but the feelings keep seeping through.

Harvey Jakes' paper had alerted the land. Its headline, "KILLER BOY TO DIE," sent the word afar.

Jenny Curran takes her time eating breakfast, her mother does not hurry her anymore. Some of her nights are still with screams, in school her classmates made up a jingle and chant it in the schoolyard in their play, she hears it now as she eats, hears them chanting:

Lori's killer goin to die,
I'll be glad when he fries.

Red Pasko and his son David are ready, they will leave at six o'clock, watch, and then come back through the night. Kevin wanted to go, but the State only permits two from a victim's family to witness executions of offenders. The youngest child, Roy, wants to go too.

Ginger Pasko is sorting clothes for her wash, she's already done all the dishes she could find to wash, cleaned everything that had a speck of dust. Lori's been dead six months, but sometimes, even during the day, she still sees her daughter, sometimes she sees her dart by the window when she's washing dishes, sees the red of her hair go by, but when she looks up it is only the open fields she sees and all her empty days come crashing back into her mind.

Megan Braxton sits with her father. If he had slept, rest did not stay on his face. He was older than she'd ever seen him, she curses the day Judge Harper called upon him to defend the undefendable. She could say nothing that would take his mind from this day. He had taken the spit from angry Banes folks, taken their "nigger-lover" slurs. His appeals failed one after the other, Supreme Mississippi Judges just shook their heads, Mississippi's Governor said "No" but he'd think about it and if he changed his mind he'd call it off. Wilbur Braxton had told Cinder, "I'll keep on trying."

Megan had pleaded with her father to let her go with him, she could wait in the car or in the small town nearby, but he'd said no. Now she is asking again.

"Daddy, I know you've said no and I know why, but I'd really like to be there with you. Please reconsider," she asks as diplomatically as she was taught.

Wilbur Braxton looks up from his desk in his home office and smiles, then says, "I truly appreciate what you're asking and giving, you've grown so much, you have in so many ways become the mother you never knew. You are like her so much." Wilbur Braxton pauses, smiles, looks at his daughter standing with the poise he admires so much, then says, "But, dear, you cannot ask me to let my children do for me things that you would never let your children do for you."

Megan understands. She gives her father what she thought he needed most, she hugs him.

In the southern tip of Greene County sits Ogin State Prison Farm and Boys Reformatory, boys twelve to fifteen are housed there until they are old enough to be transferred across the road to the adult camp. Ely Hampton had allowed Gumpy to plead guilty to second-degree murder, for which he got a twenty-year sentence. Ely Hampton had considered the testimony of Jenny Curran that Gumpy ran from the scene before the murder occurred. He also took into account that Gumpy would, as he did in his confession, name Billy as the killer and also, if need be, would testify that Billy had pulled the same knife on him.

All the boys at Ogin knew about Billy Lee Turner, many had been told they too could end up like Billy Lee Turner. They all knew the State was going to take Billy Lee Turner's life away from him at midnight tonight.

Gumpy worked in the camp's dairy-farm barn, it was stall-muckin time and he was hard at work. All morning he'd seen Billy's face, with and without the scratches, with and without his smile, with and without the dark cellblock shadows across it, then he'd see the train trestle where the Memphis train came rollin across, then he'd see the pond with its still, greenish water, then the girls would come runnin into his thoughts.

Then he would run from Billy again.

Wallace Hale is a man most folks say never smiles, just grins sometimes. Hattiesburg Prison gate guards see Wallace Hale's dusty green Packard coming and open the gate. Wallace Hale slows his car, then stops it to give his greeting, which was never much more than a nod.

"A little early, ain't ya?" the gate guard asks with a smile.

"Yeah, got some adjustments to make," Wallace Hale says with his polite grin on his face, then drives on slowly to the Death House.

Wallace Hale has reasons for his concern about adjustments he has to make. He is the executioner, it's his job to make sure the condemned man is put to death as quick and humanely as the workings of the chair allowed.

Most condemned men were of the average height and weight, some, like Jimmy Johnson and Preacher Man Sam, were extremely large or tall men, six foot two or more. Hattiesburg's was a big chair and structured for the average-sized man.

The new faces in cellblock nine are sitting in their cells and passing their morning away. Dil Martin was yellin up and down the cellblock, but now sits quietly, smiling at the silence.

Billy sits on his cot with one of the picture books he has. From moment to moment, his eyes glance from the white pages to the dark-shadowed cracks in the cell floor. Dil Martin has told him, "Hey, boy, they gonna burn yer ass till ain't nothin left but a puff of black smoke."

Billy can see the chair in his mind, sees it with fire coming out of it, sees it with Sack Man sittin in it with red-hot flames burnin him up. Sometimes he can see Jesus waiting for him, but most of the time he just sees hisself on fire till he dies.

Noon hour comes and brings Wilson Wagner. Guard Russell Vent lets the Chaplain into Billy's cell, and now he sits with Billy on his cot. Billy's quiet, not just in words and sounds, but his movements are still too. Wilson Wagner sits with him a long time before he speaks.

"Billy, ya must remember there is always hope. The Governor may call, ya know he can call anytime. Remember what faith is. Ya remember?" Wilson Wagner whispers into Billy's silence.

"Ah ain't wants ta be burns tills Ah on fire." Billy's voice trembles as he begins to quiver.

Wilson Wagner is silent.

"Theys burn ya till nothin be left, thens ya all dead."

Wilson Wagner speaks quickly, his words come strong, but gentle. "Billy, Jesus will be with ya, son."

"He catch on fire too."

"There's no fire, Billy. Ya won't catch on fire, son. It won't hurt. Jesus will be with you, nothin can hurt Jesus. Ya know that, and He's not goin to let anything hurt you. Ya know that. He loves you. Let's read now, let's read about Jesus," Wilson Wagner's voice is pleading. Now he hurries to open his Bible.

Billy sits listening to the rhythm of Wilson Wagner's words of his Jesus, they soothe his thoughts until he sees the fires again and turns away with tears.

The day's sky fades into evening gray. Food time comes, the ceremonial last supper just a candy bar and a little milk. Billy lets the hot chicken go without a touch.

He can't see the window from his cell, but knows from how the shadows fall that nighttime's come, it's dark outside. Wilson Wagner knows the hours are few.

"Billy, is there anything ya want me to tell your mother? I'm going to see her, you know," Wilson Wagner had to ask.

Billy sees Cinder and starts to cry, saying, "She can't git me. She won'ts come git me, she won't come."

"Oh, Billy," Wilson Wagner's words come low, "son, if she could, she would. God knows she would. She loves ya so much and wants you to be a big boy and be brave. She wants ya to remember about Jesus, she's asked Jesus to love you too. She's asked Jesus to be with you."

"Ah don't wants ta be electrics." Billy lifts his head and his eyes fall into Wilson Wagner's face.

Wilson Wagner closes his Bible and brings Billy into his arms, holds him close, then whispers, "Try not to think about it, son, close your eyes and think of Jesus."

Billy's quivers still, but he shakes with every stir or sound. Wilson Wagner sits holding him in the dark, sometimes thinking he's asleep, then looking down and seeing his eyes still open, just staring. In a silent prayer, that Billy does not hear, Jesus is called and Wilson Wagner tells Him it is time to come.

The cellblock lights come on, the big heavy door clanks open, Billy jerks and looks out his cell bars.

The footsteps come.

Billy jumps from Wilson Wagner's arms and runs to the corner of his cell and just stands there until the footsteps get closer, then turns his face to the cracks of the walls and tries to hide in the darkness there.

"Billy Lee Turner, it's time, son. I'm sorry, but it's time." Warden Casey Herman's voice fills Billy's cell, even the dark corners, then he motions to Guard Ed Welte to open the cell.

"Come on, boy," Ed Welte says as he opens the door, his voice is harsh. Wilson Wagner jumps to his feet and looks at the guard, saying, "For God's sakes, man." Guard Ed Welte steps back and looks at Warden Casey Herman. The warden looks at Billy in the corner and says to Wilson Wagner, "Wil, we got to get the boy out of there, he still got a little time left."

Wilson Wagner steps back and Guard Ed Welte goes into Billy's corner and grabs his arm.

"Naw, naw. Lets me go. Naw . . ." Billy screams and tries to squirm away, but Guard Ed Welte keeps pulling on his arm and yanking him into the center of the cell.

Wilson Wagner turns quickly to Warden Casey Herman, looks into his face, then turns back to Billy and Guard Ed Welte and just stands shaking his head.

"Come on, boy, come on," Guard Ed Welte keeps saying as he tries to get Billy to walk on his own.

With all his strength and will, Billy jerks and twists out of Guard Ed Welte's grasp and runs back to his corner, puts his face into the shadows, and screams, "Mama. Mama. Mama . . ."

"Git him out of there," Warden Casey Herman's voice is sharp.

"Come on, boy," Guard Ed Welte shouts and yanks Billy by the arm and starts dragging him through the cell.

"Lets me go. Ah don'ts wants ta be electrics. Lets me go. Mama. Mama," Billy screams and tries to grab on to his cot, then grab on to Wilson Wagner's legs.

"For God's sake," Wilson Wagner shouts at the warden, then quickly turns back to Billy, saying, "It's not time yet, Billy, we still have time, we're just goin to another cell. Billy, listen to me, we still have time, son, we still have time."

Guard Ed Welte yanks Billy out of the cell, then has to pry his hands off the bars he's trying to hold on to.

"Lets me go, lets me go. Ah don'ts wants ta be on fire."

Billy's screams wail through the cellblock.

"Hey, boy, hee . . . hee . . . hee . . . they gonna burn ya ass . . . hee . . . hee," Dil Martin shouts into Billy's screams.

"Shut that man up," Warden Casey Herman yells to the other night guard, Joe Ellis.

Guard Ed Welte drags Billy by the arm.

Wilson Wagner follows, Billy keeps lookin back to him.

The faces in the cells watch Billy being dragged by, the boy's cries silence the men, even Dil Martin let Billy pass without a laugh.

The door at the far end is opened by Guard Joe Ellis. Guard Ed Welte drags Billy through. Guard Joe Ellis waits until Wilson Wagner comes through, then he closes the last door of cellblock nine.

The waiting cell has a bright light, cot, but no blanket. Billy is shoved in, Wilson Wagner follows. Guard Ed Welte and Joe Ellis lock the door and stand in the walkway. Warden Casey Herman goes into the next room.

Harvey Jakes has already started taking notes, he has left Helen Marks in the main office of the prison, where she could have coffee and sit while she waits for him. He was told he could not ask questions of the prison officials during the last hour, which has begun. He stands off to the side, watching the men tinker with the straps and gadgets on the chair. Other spectators are in their seats and just watching and waiting.

Ely Hampton shakes Wilbur Braxton's hand, nods a brief greeting, says nothing else. Red Pasko and his son David sit in the front row and say nothing to anyone. Warden Casey Herman mingles with some of the official guests and makes sure to let Wilbur Braxton know his line is still open to the Governor.

As the hour eases on, the room begins to still. The lights over the rows of chairs are low-watt bulbs, beyond the hand-rail where the big chair waits the lights are brighter, giving the room a two-dimensional look.

Billy had calmed in the waiting cell, but his tears still came rolling down his cheeks as he sits on the cot listening to Wilson Wagner, and peering out through the bars at the waiting guards.

Wilson Wagner does two things, he reads from his Bible and he hopes his Jesus will really come. He knows the Governor's call isn't coming.

Billy starts looking around nervously. Wilson Wagner forces his eyes to look at the time, it is eleven-fifty. He looks at Billy, sighs, then says, "Billy, let's pray together. We can do that."

Billy remains silent, but keeps looking around.

Wilson Wagner pleads again, "Billy, let's talk to Jesus together. He wants us to."

Billy looks at Wilson Wagner, steadies his eyes, and asks, "Is Jesus be out there too? He be out theres?"

"Yes, Billy, you won't see Him, maybe you will, but He'll see you. He's there. He'll be with you, I promise you."

Wilson Wagner knows they will come soon, Guards Ed Welte and Joe Ellis begin to stir outside the cell door.

"Billy," Wilson Wagner almost shouts to get Billy's attention just on him.

Billy looks.

Wilson Wagner speaks quickly, "Billy, ya must listen, ya hear? Listen, son, for God's sake, listen to me."

Billy keeps his eyes in Wilson Wagner's eyes for a moment, but then looks away.

Wilson Wagner speaks quickly again, "Billy, just keep your eyes on me, don't look at anybody else. Just look at me and listen to my voice, Billy. Jesus is goin to tell me what to say to you, just keep your eyes on me, son, ya hear me?"

Billy keeps his eyes down to the floor until the door opens and the guards begin to open the cell.

"Naw. No . . . leaves me be. Mama. Mama. Ah don'ts wants ta be electrics." Billy's screams now shatter all the silences everywhere.

Warden Casey Herman stands at the open cell door and motions for the guards to get the prisoner.

Wilson Wagner stands and walks out into the walkway, quickly opens his Bible, and starts to read and pray.

"Naw, leave me be," Billy cries as hands grab at his shoulders and arms.

"Come on, boy," Guard Ed Welte says softly as he is pulling Billy out of the cell.

Guard Joe Ellis gets Billy's other arm and the two big guards lift and carry him to the last door.

Warden Casey Herman glances at his watch, looks behind at the two guards, nods, and opens the door.

David Pasko thought he heard someone screaming and turns when the big door opens. Warden Casey Herman enters the room slowly, then the guards come in dragging Billy, twisting and jerking in their grasp.

"Naw. Naw. Mama, Mama." His cries fill the room.

"The Lord is my shepherd, I shall not want," Wilson Wagner begins.

Billy screams with all the life he has when he sees the big dark chair sitting empty in front of the red brick wall.

David Pasko watches as the guards drag the screaming boy to the waiting chair.

Wallace Hale, the executioner, nods and says through the screams, "Hurry it up, just sit him on the edge and hold him."

Harvey Jakes writes down everything he hears.

Billy screams and jerks when he feels his body touch the big wood chair.

"Damn it, hold him still," Wallace Hale hisses as he kneels to get the leg strap around Billy's leg.

"Hurry it up," Warden Casey Herman comes forward and whispers.

Billy jerks and twist.

"Damn it, hold him still."

"He maketh me to lie down in green pastures. . . ."

"Keep him still, keep him on the edge there." Wallace Hale is tightening the leg straps.

"Naw, lets me be. Mama, Mama."

"Get his arm down, hold it, hold it right there, that's it."

The two guards and the executioner fight with Billy until they get his arms and legs strapped in the high-backed chair. Billy's feet don't reach the floor and his legs have to be strapped at the knees, his feet stick straight out towards the spectators. Now the guards try to push him back and strap his chest, but leave enough slack in the straps so the executioner can stretch the electric headpiece down to Billy's head and have enough room to adjust it.

"Just hold him there, that's it, hold him there," Wallace Hale shouts as he tries to put the metal cap on top of Billy's head, but Billy keeps jerking his head away.

"God damn it, hold his damn head."

"Can't ya get it fastened?" Guard Ed Welte asks at a whisper.

"No, damn it, slide him up."

"Thy rod and thy staff they comfort me. . . ."

"I got it now, I got it," Wallace Hale whispers.

Guards Ed Welte and Joe Ellis step back, but Wallace Hale keeps working quickly, fastening straps, connecting wires and clamps. Now he stands and moves to the side before he puts the death mask over Billy's face and pushes the gag in his mouth. He waits for the warden.

Billy lunges and strains against the straps that hold him in the chair, his legs at the knees are strapped, his arms are strapped, his chest straps are high and come under his armpits, pulling and stretching the trunk of his body against the plane of the chair so that his head can be close enough for the headset. But Billy can still scream.

Quickly, Warden Casey Herman moves and stands before Billy, he reaches into his pocket and pulls out a folded document.

Spectators and official witnesses stir nervously in their seats, but Red Pasko sits still and erect with his eyes on Billy.

"Billy Lee Turner," Warden Casey Herman begins, "having

been found guilty by the State of Mississippi of the murder of Lori Pasko on August the twenty-first of the year nineteen hundred and thirty-seven, you are hereby ordered to be put to death for that crime. Is there anything you would like to say before sentence is carried out?"

Billy's screams are trapped in his squelched chest, loud gasps come from his mouth. He can not get his breath to make words, but he still tries to call.

"Mama. Mama. Mama . . ."

Warden Casey Herman steps back quickly and nods to Wallace Hale, then says over Billy's cries, "Proceed."

Wilson Wagner prays his words and looks for Billy's eyes as he says over his cries, "Yea, though I walk through the valley of the shadow of death, I will fear no evil . . ."

Wallace Hale moves up behind Billy and straps the death mask over his face, then fidgets with its buckles to get it fastened.

Billy shakes his head as much as he can, and Wilson Wagner stops his prayers momentarily to hear Billy's cries, "Mama . . . Mama . . . Jesus . . . Jesus gits me . . ."

Wallace Hale reaches in his pocket and pulls a wad of cotton out, reaches up under Billy's death mask, and tries to get the gag into Billy's mouth. Billy clenches his teeth.

"Open up," the executioner whispers into Billy's ear, then jams the cotton through his clenched teeth.

Billy gags and gasps for air.

"Thou preparest a table before me in the presence of mine enemies. . . ."

Wallace Hale steps back quickly and looks at Warden Casey Herman.

Warden Casey Herman nods his head and the executioner goes into the generating room.

". . . and mercy shall follow me all the days of my life."

Wilson Wagner has closed his Bible and stands with his head bowed, but keeps praying, "Jesus is Christ, Saviour of Man, please accept the child into Your heavenly kingdom. . . ."

Billy chokes and gasps in the dark of his death mask. Then his mind bursts open, his thoughts spark and catch fire, he shakes and flies into the air and jolts when the straps jerk him back. The loose-fitting death mask flies from his face. David Pasko turns away.

Ely Hampton bows his head when he sees tears fling away from the twisted face.

Billy sits limp in the chair, his eyes popped open and protruding from his face.

The electric generator whines and the static crackling sound pierces the room again. Billy's body jolts upwards again, shakes and quivers in the air, then falls back to its seat and stills.

Warden Casey Herman waits a moment, then walks up to Billy and looks down into his face. He nods and a man comes up to Billy's side, puts his hand on Billy's neck, leans over him and places a stethoscope on his chest, listens a moment before he turns to the warden and says, "I pronounce this boy legally dead."

Billy lays limp in the chair, his face and head still smoking from the fires that burned his body and soul.

Harvey Jakes' nostrils begin to twitch, the stench of burnt flesh seeps into his smell, he turns from Billy's bulging eyes and tries to get away from the pungent odor. He retches and the dinner he had with Helen Marks comes up on his shirt and tie.

Red Pasko sits still and stares at the body, but sees Lori laying dead in his bed, sees her running and laughing, then sees her dead again, and keeps his eyes on the limp body sagging in the chair.

Wilbur Braxton stands up and walks to the back of the room and takes the handkerchief from his pocket and wipes the tears from his eyes.

Guards Ed Welte and Joe Ellis begin to unstrap Billy from the chair as two other guards bring in the prison coffin box.

Wilson Wagner has kept his head bowed, but still prays, silently.

Sighs and heavy breathing still fill the room. David Pasko nudges his father and whispers, "It's over now." Red Pasko does not move.

Billy is lifted from the chair and dropped in the box.

Time crept away, the midnight hour grew cold.

Cinder had watched the night, sat and stared out into it from her window. There were no words she could say, she just kept her eyes on Billy, seen his face a million times, kept looking for it and reaching for it until she screamed out into the night. Patch dogs barked and howled, Reverend Sims prayed to his God, ask Him to come to this child, reach His hands around her, and ease her pain. He'd called all the words he knew, said, "Dear God, take the pain from this woman's soul. Dear God, have mercy in this night, give eyes to the dark, let it see its evil ways, let it see how it has gone astray."

Cinder sat and cried all night.

Mississippi's sky stayed dark.